THE AUTHENTIC LIFE OF BILLY, THE KID

THE AUTHENTIC LIFE OF

BILLY, THE KID

The Noted Desperado of the Southwest, Whose Deeds of Daring and Blood made His Name A Terror in New Mexico, Arizona and Northern Mexico

By
Pat F. Garrett

Sheriff of Lincoln Co., N.M., By Whom He Was Finally Hunted Down and Captured By Killing Him

KALPAZ

ISBN: 978-93-5128-371-3(HB)

First Published in 1882
Indian Reprint in 2017

Published by

Kalpaz Publications
C-30, Satyawati Nagar,
Delhi – 110052
E-mail: kalpaz@hotmail.com
Website: kalpazpublications.com
Ph.: +91-9212142040

Cataloging in Publication Data—DK
Courtesy: D.K. Agencies (P) Ltd. <docinfo@dkagencies.com>

Garrett, Pat F. (Pat Floyd), 1850-1908, **author.**
The authentic life of Billy, the kid : the noted desperado of the Southwest, whose deeds of daring and blood made his name a terror in New Mexico, Arizona and northern Mexico / by Pat F. Garrett.
pages cm
"First published in 1882"
ISBN 9789351283713 (HB)

1. Billy, the Kid. 2. Outlaws—Southwest, New—Biography. 3. Frontier and pioneer life—Southwest, New. 4. Southwest, New—Biography. 5. Southwest, New—History—1848- I. Title.

F786.B54G37 2017 DDC 364.1552092 23

The Authentic Life of Billy, The Kid

The Noted Desperado of the Southwest, Whose Deeds of Daring and Blood made His Name A Terror in New Mexico, Arizona and Northern Mexico

By Pat F. Garrett

Sheriff of Lincoln Co., N.M.,
By Whom He Was Finally Hunted Down and Captured By Killing Him

A Faithful and Interesting Narrative

SANTA FE, NEW MEXICO
NEW MEXICAN PRINTING AND PUBLISHING CO.
1882

INTRODUCTORY

Yielding to repeated solicitations from various sources, I have addressed myself to the task of compiling, for publication, a true history of the life, adventures, and tragic death of William H. Bonney, better known as "Billy The Kid," whose daring deeds and bloody crimes have excited, for some years last past, the wonder of one-half of the world, and the admiration or detestation of the other half.

I am incited to this labor, in a measure, by an impulse to correct the thousand false statements which have appeared in the public newspapers and in yellow-covered, cheap novels. Of the latter, no less than three have been foisted upon the public, any one of which might have been the history of any outlaw who ever lived, but were miles from correct as applied to "The Kid." These pretend to disclose his name, the place of his nativity, the particulars of his career, the circumstances which drove him to his desperate life, detailing a hundred impossible deeds of reckless crime of which he was never guilty, and in localities which he never visited.

I would dissever "The Kid's" memory from that of meaner villains, whose deeds have been attributed to him. I will strive to do justice to his character, give him credit for all the virtues he possessed—and he was by no means devoid of virtue—but shall not spare deserved opprobrium for his heinous offenses against humanity and the laws.

I have known "The Kid" personally since and during the continuance of what was known as "The Lincoln County War," up to the moment of his death, of which I was the unfortunate instrument, in the discharge of my official duty. I have listened, at camp-fires, on the trail, on the prairies and at many different plazas, to his disconnected relations of events of his early and more recent life. In gathering correct information, I have interviewed many persons—since "The Kid's" death—with whom he was intimate and to whom he conversed freely of his affairs, and I am in daily intercourse with one friend who was a boarder at the house of "The Kid's" mother, at Silver City, N. M., in 1873. This man has known Bonney well from that time to his death, and has traced his career carefully and not with indifference. I have communicated, by letter, with various reliable parties, in New York, Kansas, Colorado, New Mexico, Arizona, Texas, Chihuahua, Sonora, and other states of Mexico, in order to catch up any missing links in his life, and can safely guarantee that the reader will find in my little book a true and concise relation of the principal interesting events therein, without exaggeration or excusation.

I make no pretension to literary ability, but propose to give to the public in intelligible English, "a round, unvarnished tale," unadorned with superfluous verbiage. The truth, in the life of young Bonney, needs no pen dipped in blood to thrill the heart and stay its pulsations. Under the *nom de guerre* "The Kid," his most bloody and desperate deeds were wrought—a name which will live in the annals of daring crime so long as those of Dick Turpin and Claude Duval shall be remembered. Yet, a hundred volumes have been written, exhausting the imagination of a dozen authors—authors whose stock in trade was vivid imagination—to immortalize these two latter. This verified history of "The Kid's" exploits, devoid of exaggeration, exhibits him the peer of any fabled brigand on record, unequalled in desperate courage, presence of mind in danger, devotion to his allies, generosity to his foes, gallantry, and all the elements which appeal to the holier emotions, whilst those who would revel in pictured scenes of slaughter may batten until their morbid appetites are surfeited on bloody frays and mortal encounters, unaided by fancy or the pen of fiction.

Risking the charge of prolixity, I wish to add a few words to this, my address to the public, *vide*, a sermon (among many others), recently preached in an eastern city by an eminent divine, of which discourse "The Kid" was the literal, if not the announced text.

Although I do not propose to offer my readers a sensational novel, yet, they will find it no Sunday school homily, holding up "The Kid" as an example of God's vengeance to sinful youth. The fact that he lied, swore, gambled, and broke the Sabbath in his childhood, only proved that youth and exuberant humanity were rife in the child. He but emulated thousands of his predecessors, who lived to manhood and died honored and revered—some for public and some for domestic virtues, some for their superior intellect, and many more for their wealth—how attained the world will never pause to inquire. "The Kid's" career of crime was not the outgrowth of an evil disposition, nor was it caused by unchecked youthful indiscretions; it was the result of untoward, unfortunate circumstances acting upon a bold, reckless, ungoverned, and ungovernable spirit, which no physical restraint could check, no danger appal, and no power less potent than death could conquer.

The sentiments involved in the sermon alluded to are as antedeluvian in monotonous argument, language, and sense, as the Blue Laws of Connecticut. Sabbath-breaking was the sole and inevitable cause of "The Kid's" murders, robberies and bloody death(?). Immaculate mentor of the soul. "The Kid" never knew when Sunday came here on the frontier, except by accident, and yet, he knew as much about it as some hundreds of other young men who enjoy the reputation of model youth. And, suppose "The Kid" had knowingly violated the Sabbath? He had Christ and his disciples as holy examples—confining his depredations, however, to rounding up a bunch of cattle, not his own, instead of making a raid on his neighbor's corn field and purloining roasting ears.

"The Kid" had a lurking devil in him; it was a good-humored, jovial imp, or a cruel and blood-thirsty fiend, as circumstances prompted. Circumstances favored the worser angel, and "The Kid" fell.

A dozen affidavits have been proffered me for publication, in verification of the truth of my work. I have refused them all with thanks. Let those doubt who will.

PAT F. GARRETT.

CHAPTER I.

Parentage, Nativity, Childhood, and Youth—Prophetic Symptoms at Eight Years of Age—Model Young Gentleman—Defender of the Helpless—A Mother—"Holy Nature"—A Young Bruiser—First Taste of Blood—A Fugitive—Farewell Home and a Mother's Influence

William H. Bonney, the hero of this history, was born in the city of New York, November 23d, 1859.

But little is known of his father, as he died when Billy was very young, and he had little recollection of him. In 1862 the family, consisting of the father, mother, and two boys, of whom Billy was the eldest, emigrated to Coffeyville, Kansas. Soon after settling there the father died, and the mother with her two boys removed to Colorado, where she married a man named Antrim, who is said to be now living at, or near, Georgetown, in Grant County, New Mexico, and is the only survivor of the family of four, who removed to Santa Fe, New Mexico, shortly after the marriage. Billy was then four or five years of age.

These facts are all that can be gleaned of Billy's early childhood, which, up to this time, would be of no interest to the reader.

Antrim remained at and near Santa Fe for some years, or until Billy was about eight years of age.

It was here that the boy exhibited a spirit of reckless daring, yet generous and tender feeling, which rendered him the darling of his young companions in his gentler moods, and their terror when the angry fit was on him. It was here that he became adept at cards and noted among his comrades as successfully aping the genteel vices of his elders.

It has been said that at this tender age he was convicted of larceny in Santa Fe, but as a careful examination of the court records of that city fail to support the rumor, and as Billy, during all his after life, was never charged with a little meanness or petty crime, the statement is to be doubted.

About the year 1868, when Billy was eight or nine years of age, Antrim again removed and took up his residence at Silver City, in Grant County, New Mexico. From this date to 1871, or until Billy was twelve years old, he exhibited no characteristics prophesying his desperate and disastrous future. Bold, daring, and reckless, he was open-handed, generous-hearted, frank, and manly. He was a favorite with all classes and ages, especially was he loved and admired by the old and decrepit, and the young and helpless. To such he was a champion, a defender, a benefactor, a right arm. He was never seen to accost a lady, especially an elderly one, but with his hat in his hand, and did her attire or appearance evidence poverty, it was a poem to see the eager, sympathetic, deprecating look in Billy's sunny face, as he proffered assistance or afforded information. A little child never lacked a lift across a gutter, or the assistance of a strong arm to carry a heavy burden when Billy was in sight.

To those who knew his mother, his courteous, kindly, and benevolent spirit was no mystery. She was evidently of Irish descent. Her husband called her Kathleen. She was about the medium height, straight, and graceful in form, with regular features, light blue eyes, and luxuriant golden hair. She was not a beauty, but what the world calls a fine-looking woman. She kept boarders in Silver City, and her charity and goodness of heart were proverbial. Many a hungry "tenderfoot" has had cause to bless the fortune which led him to her door. In all her deportment she exhibited the unmistakable characteristics of a lady—a lady by instinct and education.

Billy loved his mother. He loved and honored her more than anything else on earth. Yet his home was not a happy one to him. He has often declared that the tyranny and cruelty of his step-father drove him from home and a mother's influence, and that Antrim was responsible for his going to the bad. However this may be, after the death of his mother, some four years since, the step-father would have been unfortunate had he come in contact with his eldest stepson.

Billy's educational advantages were limited, as were those of all of the youth of this border country. He attended public school, but acquired more information at his mother's knee than from the village pedagogue. With great natural intelligence and an active brain, he became a fair scholar. He wrote a fair letter, was a tolerable arithmetician, but beyond this he did not aspire.

The best and brightest side of Billy's character has been portrayed above. The shield had another side never exhibited to his best friends—the weak and helpless. His temper was fearful, and in his angry moods he was dangerous. He was not loud or swaggering, or boisterous. He never threatened. He had no bark, or, if he did, the bite came first. He never took advantage of an antagonist, but barring size and weight, would, when aggrieved, fight any man in Silver City. His misfortune was, he could not and would not stay whipped. When oversized and worsted in a fight, he sought such arms as he could buy, borrow, beg, or steal, and used them, upon more than one occasion, with murderous intent.

During the latter portion of Billy's residence in Silver City, he was the constant companion of Jesse Evans, a mere boy, but as daring and dangerous as many an older and more experienced desperado. He was older than Billy and constituted himself a sort of preceptor to our hero. These two were destined to jointly participate in many dangerous adventures, many narrow escapes, and several bloody affrays in the next few years, and, fast friends as they now were, the time was soon to come when they would be arrayed in opposition to one another, each thirsting for the other's blood, and neither shrinking from the conflict. They parted at Silver City, but only to meet again many times during Billy's short and bloody career.

When young Bonney was about twelve years of age, he first imbrued his hand in human blood. This affair, it may be said, was the turning point in his life, outlawed him, and gave him over a victim of his worser impulses and passions.

As Billy's mother was passing a knot of idlers on the street, a filthy loafer in the crowd made an insulting remark about her. Billy heard it and quick as thought, with blazing eyes, he planted a stinging blow on the blackguard's mouth, then springing to the street, stooped for a rock. The brute made a rush for him, but as he passed Ed. Moulton, a well-known citizen of Silver City, he received a stunning blow on the ear which felled him, whilst Billy was caught and restrained. However, the punishment inflicted on the offender by no means satisfied Billy. Burning for revenge, he visited a miner's cabin, procured a Sharp's rifle, and started in search of his intended victim. By good fortune, Moulton saw him with the gun, and, with some difficulty, persuaded him to return it.

Some three weeks subsequent to this adventure, Moulton, who was a wonderfully powerful and active man, skilled in the art of self-defense, and with something of the prize-fighter in his composition, became involved in a rough-and-tumble bar-room fight, at Joe Dyer's saloon. He had two shoulder-strikers to contend with and was getting the best of both of them, when Billy's "antipathy"—the man who had been the recipient of one of Moulton's "lifters," standing by, thought he saw an opportunity to take cowardly revenge on

Moulton, and rushed upon him with a heavy bar-room chair upraised. Billy was usually a spectator, when not a principal, to any fight which might occur in the town, and this one was no exception. He saw the motion, and like lightning darted beneath the chair-once, twice, thrice, his arm rose and fell—then, rushing through the crowd, his right hand above his head, grasping a pocket-knife, its blade dripping with gore, he went out into the night, an outcast and a wanderer, a murderer, self-baptized in human blood. He went out like banished Cain, yet less fortunate than the first murderer, there was no curse pronounced against his slayer. His hand was now against every man, and every man's hand against him. He went out forever from the care, the love, and influence of a fond mother, for he was never to see her face again—she who had so lovingly reared him, and whom he had so tenderly and reverently loved. Never more shall her soft hand smooth his ruffled brow, whilst soothing words charm from his swelling heart the wrath he nurses. No mentor, no love to restrain his evil passion or check his desperate hand—what must be his fate?

Billy did, truly, love and revere his mother, and all his after life of crime was marked by deep devotion and respect for good women, born, doubtless, of his adoration for her.

"* * * * *from earlier than I know,
Immersed in rich foreshadowing of the world,
I loved the woman; he that doth not, lives
A drowning life, besotted in sweet self,
Or pines in sad experience worse than death,
Or keeps his winged affections clipt with crime;
Yet, was there one through whom I loved her, one
Not learned, save in gracious household ways,
Not perfect, nay, but full of tender wants,
No angel, but a dearer being, all dipt
In angel instincts, breathing Paradise,
Interpreter between the Gods and men,
Who looked all native to her place, and yet
On tiptoe seemed to touch upon a sphere
Too gross to tread, and all male minds perforce
Swayde to her from their orbits, as they moved
And girdled her with music. Happy he
With such a mother! Faith in womankind
Beats with his blood, and trust in all things high
Comes easy to him, and though he trip and fall,
He shall not blind his soul with clay."

Alas! for Billy. All the good influences were withdrawn from his patch. The dove of peace and good will to his kind could find no resting place in his mind, distorted by fiery passion, and when deadly revenge shook his soul, he would have plucked the messenger from its perch, "though her jesses were his heartstrings." He tripped and fell: he soiled his soul with clay.

CHAPTER II.

Steals His First Horse—Finds a Partner—Kills Three Indians for Plunder—A Star Gambler in Arizona—High Times in Tucson—Horse Race with Indian—No Show to Lose—A Tight Place—Killing at Fort Bowie, and Flight from Arizona—Old Mexico

And now we trace our fugitive to Arizona. His deeds of desperate crime in that Territory are familiar to old residents there but it is impossible to follow them in detail, or to give exact dates. It is probable that many of his lawless achievements have escaped both written history and tradition. Records of the courts, at the Indian agency and military posts, and reports from officers and citizens give all the information which can be obtained and cover his most prominent exploits. These reports tally correctly with Billy's disconnected recitals, as given to his companions, in after years, to pass away an idle hour.

After the fateful night when Billy first imbrued his hands in blood and fled his home, he wandered for three days and nights without meeting a human being except one Mexican sheepherder. He talked Spanish as fluently as any Mexican of them all, and secured from this boy a small stock of provisions, consisting of *tortillas* and mutton. He was on foot, and trying to make his way to the Arizona line. Becoming bewildered, he made a circuit and returned to the vicinity of McKnight's ranch, where he took his initiatory in horse-stealing.

The next we hear of Billy, some three weeks after his departure from Silver City, he arrived at Fort (then Camp) Bowie, Arizona, with a companion, both mounted on one sore-backed pony, equipped with a pack-saddle and rope bridle, without a quarter of a dollar between them, nor a mouthful of provision in the commissary.

Billy's partner doubtless had a name which was his legal property, but he was so given to changing it that it was impossible to fix on the right one. Billy always called him "*Alias.*"

With a fellow of Billy's energy and peculiar ideas as to the rights of property, this condition of impoverishment could not continue. After recuperating his enervated physique at the Fort, he and his companion, on foot (having disposed of their pony), with one condemned rifle and one pistol, borrowed from soldiers, started out on Billy's first unlawful raid.

As is generally known, Fort Bowie is in Pima County, Arizona, and on the Chiracahua Apache Indian Reservation. These Indians were peaceable and quiet at this time, and there was no danger in trusting one's self amongst them. Billy and his companion fell in with a party of three of these Indians, some eight or ten miles southwest of Fort Bowie in the passes of the mountains. A majority of the different tribes of Apaches speak Spanish, and Billy was immediately at home with these. His object was to procure a mount for himself and his companion. He tried arguments, wheedling, promises to pay, and every other plan his prolific brain could suggest—all in vain. These Indians' confidence in white man's reliability had been severely shaken in the person of Indian Agent Clum.

Billy gave a vague account of the result of this enterprise, yet uncompromising as it sounds, it leaves little to surmise. Said he:

"It was a ground hog case. Here were twelve good ponies, four or five saddles, a good supply of blankets, and five pony loads of pelts. Here were three blood-thirsty savages, revelling in all this luxury and refusing succor to two free-born, white American citizens, foot sore and hungry. The plunder had to change hands—there was no alternative—and as one live Indian could place a hundred United States troops on our trail in two hours, and as a dead Indian would be likely to take some other route, our resolves were taken. In three minutes there were three "good Injuns" lying around there, careless like, and, with ponies and plunder, we skipped. There was no fight. It was about the softest thing I ever struck."

The movements of these two youthful brigands for a few days subsequent to the killing of these Indians are lost sight of. It is known that they disposed of superfluous ponies, equipage, and furs to immigrants from Texas, more than a hundred miles distant from Fort Bowie, and that they returned to the reservation splendidly mounted and armed, with money in their pockets. They were on the best of terms with government officials and citizens at Fort Bowie, Apache Pass, San Simon, San Carlos, and all the settlements in that vicinity, and spent a good deal of their time at Tucson, where Billy's skill as a monte dealer and card player generally kept the two boys in luxuriant style and gave them enviable prestige among the sporting fraternity, which was then a powerful and influential element in Arizona.

If anything was known by the authorities, of the Indian killing episode, nothing was done about it. No one regretted the loss of these Indians, and no money could be made by prosecuting the offenders.

The quiet life Billy led in the plazas palled upon his senses, and, with his partner, he again took the road, or rather the mountain trails. There was always a dash of humor in Billy's most tragical adventures. Meeting a band of eight or ten Indians in the vicinity of San Simon, the two young fellows proposed and instituted a horse-race. Billy was riding a very superior animal, but made the race and bets on the inferior one ridden by his partner, against the best horse the Indians had. He also insisted that his partner should hold the stakes, consisting of money and revolvers.

Billy was to ride. Mounting his partner's horse, the word was given, and three, instead of two, horses shot out from the starting point. The interloper was Billy's partner, on Billy's horse. He could not restrain the fiery animal, which flew the track, took the bit in his teeth, and never slackened his headlong speed until he reached a deserted cattle ranch, many miles away from the improvised race track.

Billy lost the race, but who was the winner? His partner with all the stakes, was macadamizing the rocky trails, far beyond their ken, and far beyond successful pursuit. It required all Billy's Spanish eloquence, all his persuasive powers of speech and gesture, all his sweetest, most appealing expressions of infantile innocence, to convince the untutored and unreasoning savages that he, himself, was not only the greatest loser of them all, but that he was the victim of the perfidy of a traitor—to them a heinous crime. Had not he, Billy, taken all the bets, and lost them all? Whilst their loss was divided between a half-dozen, he had lost his horse, his arms, his money, his friends and his confidence in humanity, with nothing to show for it but an old plug of a pony that evidently could not win a race against a lame *burro*.

When did youth and good looks, with well simulated injured innocence, backed by eloquence of tongue and hand-spiced with grief and righteous anger, fail to affect, even an Apache. With words of condolence and encouragement from his sympathizing victims, Billy rode sadly away. Two days thereafter, a hundred miles from thence, Billy might have been seen solemnly dividing spoils with his fugitive friend.

The last and darkest deed of which Billy was guilty in Arizona was the killing of a soldier blacksmith at Fort Bowie. The date and particulars of this killing are not upon record, and Billy was always reticent in regard to it. There are many conflicting rumors in regard thereto. Billy's defenders justify him on the ground that the victim was a bully, refused to yield up money fairly won from him, by Billy, in a game of cards, and precipitated his fate by attempting to inflict physical chastisement on a beardless boy. One thing is sure, this deed exiled Billy from Arizona, and he is next heard of in the State of Sonora, Republic of Mexico.

CHAPTER III.

Gay Life in Sonora—Killing of Don Jose Martinez—Taking Desperate Chances—Nerves of Steel—A Loud Call for Life—Deadly Aim—Cool as a Cucumber—A Ride for Life and Lucky Escape

In Sonora, Billy's knowledge of the Spanish language, and his skill in all games of cards practiced by the Mexican people, at once established for him a reputation as a first class gambler and high-toned gentleman. All that is known of his career in Sonora is gathered from his own relation of casual events, without detail or dates. He went there alone, but soon established a coalition with a young Mexican gambler, named Melquiades Segura, which lasted during his stay in the Republic.

There is but one fatal encounter, of which we have official evidence, charged against Billy during his sojourn in Sonora, and this necessitated his speedy and permanent change of base. This was the killing of Don Jose Martinez, a monte dealer, over a gaming table. Martinez had, for some weeks, persistently followed a course of bullying and insult towards Billy, frequently refusing to pay him money fairly won at his game. Billy's entrance to the club-room was a signal for Martinez to open his money drawer, take out a six shooter, lay it on the table beside him, and commence a tirade of abuse directed against "Gringos" generally, and Billy in particular.

There could be but one termination to this difficulty. Billy settled his affairs in the plaza, he and Segura saddled their horses, and about nine o'clock at night rode into a *placita* having two outlets, hard by the club-room. Leaving Segura with the horses, Billy visited the gambling house.

The insult came as was expected. Billy's pistol was in the scabbard. Martinez had his on the table and under his hand. Before putting his hand on his pistol the warning came from Billy's lips, in steady tones: "Jose, do you fight as bravely with that pistol as you do with your mouth?" and his hand fell on the butt of his pistol. And here Billy exhibited that lightning rapidity, iron nerve, and marvellous skill with a pistol, which gave him such advantage over antagonists, and rendered his name a terror, even to adepts in pistol practice.

Martinez was no coward but he counted too much on his advantage. The two pistols exploded as one, and Martinez fell back in his seat, dead, shot through the eye. Billy slapped his left hand to his right ear, as though he were reaching for a belligerent mosquito. He said, afterwards, that it felt as though some one had caught three or four hairs and jerked them out.

Before it was fairly realized that Martinez was dead, two horsemen were rushing across the *cienega* which lies between the plaza and the mountains, and Billy had shaken the dust of Sonora from his feet, forever.

A party of about twenty Mexicans started immediately in pursuit, which they held steadily for more than ten days. They found the horses ridden from the plaza by Billy and Segura, but horses were plenty to persons of such persuasive manners as the fugitives. The chase was fruitless and the pursuers returned to Sonora.

The family of Martinez offered a large reward for the apprehension and return of Billy to Sonora, and a lesser one for Segura. Several attempts were subsequently made, by emissaries of the family, to inveigle Billy back there. The bait was too thin.

CHAPTER IV.

Chihuahua City—Bad Luck—His Fate Follows Him in Shape of a Dead Monte Dealer and a Sack of Doubloons—"Holding Up" Billy's Bank—Adios Chihuahua

After their flight from Sonora, Billy and Segura made their way to the city of Chihuahua, where their usual good luck at cards deserted them. Billy appeared, unconsciously, to make enemies of the gambling fraternity there. Perhaps a little envy of his skill, his powers, and his inimitable nonchalant style had something to do with it.

His difficulties culminated one night. Billy had won a considerable sum of money at a monte table when the dealer closed his bank and sneeringly informed Billy that he did not have money enough in his bank to pay his losses, whilst he was, at that moment, raking doubloons and double doubloons into a buckskin sack—money enough to pay Billy a dozen times over, leering at Billy the meanwhile.

Billy made no reply, but he and Segura left the house. That monte dealer never reached home with his sack of gold, and his peon, who was carrying the sack, now lives on the Rio Grande, in New Mexico, in comparatively affluent circumstances.

Billy and his partner were seen no more, publicly, on the streets of Chihuahua City, but three other prosperous monte dealers were mysteriously "held up," at night, as they were returning home from the club-rooms, and each was relieved of his wealth. It was afterwards remarked that each of these men had offended Billy or Segura. The gamblers speculated at large upon the mysterious disappearance of the dealer who had so openly and defiantly robbed Billy, and they and his family mourn him as dead. Perhaps they do so with cause.

The two adventurers concluded that Chihuahua was not the heaven they were seeking, and vanished. Their further movements will be reserved for another chapter, but it may be in place to remark that for some months thereafter, the boys settled their little bills along their sinuous route, in Spanish gold, by drafts on a buckskin sack, highly wrought in gold and silver thread and lace, in the highest style of Mexican art.

As to the monte dealer who so suddenly disappeared, although Billy never disclosed the particulars of the affair, recent advices from Chihuahua give the assurance that the places which knew him there have known him no more since that eventful night.

CHAPTER V.

A Wanderer—Jesse Evans, Again—Billy's Appearance at Seventeen Years of Age—Billy and Jess—Volunteer in a Fight against the Mescaleros—Bloody Work—Slaughtering Indians with an Ax

After leaving Chihuahua, Billy and Segura went to the Rio Grande, where they parted company, but only for a short time. Up to the month of December, 1876, Billy's career was erratic, and it is impossible to follow his adventures consecutively; many of them are, doubtless, lost to history. He fell in again with his old companion, Jesse Evans, and all that is known of Billy's exploits during the ensuing few months is gained by his own and Jesse's disconnected narrations.

This youthful pair made themselves well known in Western Texas, Northern and Eastern Mexico, and along the Rio Grande in New Mexico by a hundred deeds of daring crime. Young Jess. had already won for himself the reputation of a brave but unscrupulous desperado, and in courage and skill with deadly weapons, he and Billy were fairly matched. They were, at this time, of nearly the same size. Jess. was, probably, a year or two the oldest, whilst Billy was, slightly, the tallest, and a little heavier. Billy was seventeen years of age in November, 1876, and was nearly as large as at the day of his death. A light brown beard was beginning to show up on his lip and cheeks; his hair was of a darker brown, glossy, and luxuriant; his eyes were a deep blue, dotted with spots of a hazel hue, and were very bright, expressive, and intelligent. His face was oval in form, the most noticeable feature being two projecting upper front teeth, which knowing newspaper correspondents, who never saw the man nor the scenes of his adventures, describe as "fangs which gave to his features an intensely cruel and murderous expression." Nothing can be further from the truth. That these teeth were a prominent feature in his countenance is true; that when he engaged in conversation, or smiled they were noticeable is true; but they did not give to his always pleasing expression a cruel look, nor suggest either murder or treachery. All who ever knew Billy will testify that his polite, cordial, and gentlemanly bearing invited confidence and promised protection—the first of which he never betrayed, and the latter he was never known to withhold. Those who knew him best will tell you that in his most savage and dangerous moods his face always wore a smile. He ate and laughed, drank and laughed, rode and laughed, talked and laughed, fought and laughed, and killed and laughed. No loud and boisterous guffaw, but a pleasant smile or a soft and musical "ripple of the voice." Those who knew him watched his eyes for an exhibition of anger. Had his biographers stated that the expression of his eyes—to one who could read them—in angry mood was cruel and murderous, they would have shown a more perfect knowledge of the man. One could scarcely believe that those blazing, baleful orbs and that laughing face could be controlled by the same spirit.

Billy was, at this time, about five feet seven and one half inches high, straight as a dart, weighed about one hundred and thirty-five pounds, and was as light, active, and graceful as a panther. His form was well-knit, compact, and wonderfully muscular. It was his delight, when he had a misunderstanding with one larger and more powerful than himself, but who feared him on account of his skill with weapons, to unbuckle his belt, drop his arms, and say: "Come on old fellow: I've got no advantage now. Let's fight it out, knuckles and skull." He usually won his fights; if he got the worst of it, he bore no malice.

There were no bounds to his generosity. Friends, strangers, and even his enemies, were welcome to his money, his horse, his clothes, or anything else of which he happened, at the time, to be possessed. The aged, the poor, the sick, the unfortunate and helpless never appealed to Billy in vain for succor.

There is an impression among some people that Billy was excessively gross, profane, and beastly in his habits, conversation, and demeanor. The opposite is the case. A majority of the "too tooist," "uttermost, utterly utter," "curled darlings" of society might take example by Billy's courteous and gentlemanly demeanor, to their own great improvement and the relief of disgusted sensible men. It would be strange, with Billy's particular surroundings, if he did not indulge in profanity. He did; but his oaths were expressed in the most elegant phraseology, and, if purity of conversation were the test, hundreds of the prominent citizens of New Mexico would be taken for desperadoes sooner than young Bonney.

Billy was, when circumstances permitted, scrupulously neat and elegant in dress. Some newspaper correspondents have clothed him in fantastic Italian brigand or Mexican guerrilla style, with some hundreds of dollars worth of gold lace, etc., ornamenting his dress; but they did not so apparel him with his consent. His attire was, usually, of black, a black frock coat, dark pants and vest, a neat boot to his small, shapely foot, and (his only noticeable peculiarity in dress) usually, a Mexican sombrero. He wore this for convenience, not for show. They are very broad-brimmed, protecting the face from the sun, wind, and dust, and very durable. They are expensive, but Billy never owned one which cost hundreds of dollars. They are worth, in Chihuahua, from $10 to $50. Some silly fellow, with a surplus of money and paucity of brains, may have loaded his hat with a thousand dollars worth of medals, gold lace, and thread, but Billy was not of those.

Billy and Jess. put in the few months they spent together by indulging in a hundred lawless raids—sometimes committing depredations in Mexico and fleeing across the Rio Grande into Texas or

New Mexico, and vice versa, until hundreds of ranchmen, in both republics were on the look out for them, and in many conflicts, on either side of the river, they escaped capture, and consequent certain death, almost by miracle. There was no mountain so high, no precipice so steep, no torrent so fierce, no river so swift, no cave so deep, but these two would essay it in their daring rides for liberty. More than one bold pursuer bit the dust in these encounters, and a price was offered for the bodies of the outlaws, dead or alive.

The Mescalero Apache Indians, from the Fort Stanton, New Mexico, Reservation, used to make frequent raids into Old Mexico, and often attacked emigrants along the Rio Grande. On one occasion, a party from Texas, consisting of three men and their families, on their way to Arizona, came across Billy and Jess. in the vicinity of the Rio Miembres. They took dinner together and the Texans volunteered much advice to the two unsophisticated boys, representing the danger they braved by travelling unprotected through an Indian country, and proposing that they should pursue their journey in company. They represented themselves as old and experienced Indian fighters, who had, in Texas, scored their hundreds of dead Comanches, Kickapoos, and Lipans. The boys declined awaiting the slow motion of ox wagons, and after dinner, rode on.

About the middle of the afternoon, the boys discovered a band of Indians moving along the foot-hills on the south, in an easterly direction. They speculated on the chances of their new friends, the emigrants, falling in with these Indians, until, from signs of a horse's footprints, they became convinced that an Indian messenger had preceded them from the east, and putting that and that together, it was evident to them that the band of Indians they had seen were bent on no other mission than to attack the emigrants.

With one impulse the young knights wheeled their horses and struck across the prairie to the foot-hills to try and cut the Indian trail. This they succeeded in doing, and found that the party consisted of fourteen warriors, who were directing their course so as to surely intercept the emigrants, or strike them in camp. The weary horses caught the spirit of their brave riders, and over rocks and hills, through cañons and tule break the steady measured thud of their hoofs alone broke the silence.

"Can we make it, Billy?" queried Jess. "Will our horses hold out?"

"The question isn't, will we? but how soon?" replied Billy. "It's a ground hog case. We've got to get there. Think of those white-headed young ones, Jess., and whoop up. When my horse's four legs let up, I've got two of my own."

Just at dusk the brave boys rounded a point in the road and came in full view of the emigrant's camp. In time—just in time. At this very moment the terrible yell of the Apache broke upon their ears, and the savage band charged the camp from a pass on the south. The gallant horses which had carried the boys so bravely were reeling in their tracks. Throwing themselves out of the saddles, the young heroes grasped their Winchesters and on a run, with a yell as blood-curdling as any red devil of them all could utter, they threw themselves amongst the yelling fiends. There was astonishment and terror in the tone which answered the boys' war cry, and the confusion amongst the reds increased as one after another of their number went down under the unerring aim of the two rifles. Jess. had stumbled and fallen into a narrow arroyo, overgrown with tall grass and weeds. Raising himself to his knees, he found that his fall was a streak of great good luck. As he afterwards remarked he could not have made a better intrenchment if he had worked a week. Calling Billy, he plied his Winchester rapidly. When Billy saw the favorable position Jess. had involuntarily fallen into, he bounded into it; but just as he dropped to his knees a ball from an Indian rifle shattered the stock of his Winchester and the broken wood inflicted a painful wound on Billy's hand. His gun useless, he fought with his six-shooter-fuming and cursing his luck.

The boys could not see what was going on in the camp, as a wagon intervened; but soon Billy heard the scream of a child as if in death-agony, and the simultaneous shriek of a woman. Leaping from his intrenchment, he called to Jess. to stay there and cover his attack, whilst he sprang away, pistol in one hand and a small Spanish dagger in the other, directly towards the camp. At this moment the Indians essayed to drive them from their defense. Billy met them more than half way and fought his way through a half-dozen of them. He had emptied his revolver, and had no time to load it. Clubbing his pistol he rushed on, and, dodging a blow from a burly Indian, he darted under a wagon and fell on a prairie axe.

Billy afterwards said he believed that his howl of delight frightened those Indians so that he and Jess. won the fight. He emerged on the other side of the wagon. A glance showed him the three men and all the women and children but one woman and one little girl, ensconced behind the other two wagons, and partly protected by a jutting rock. One woman and the little girl were lying, apparently lifeless, on the ground. With yell on yell Billy fell among the reds with his axe. He never missed hearing every crack of Jess' rifle, and in three minutes there was not a live Indian in sight. Eight "good" ones slept their last sleep. Billy's face, hands, and clothing, the wagons, the camp furniture, and the grass were bespattered with blood and brains.

Turning to the campers, the boys discovered that the little girl had received a fracture of the skull in an attempt, by an Indian brave, to brain her, and the mother had fainted. All three of the men were wounded. One was shot through the abdomen and in the shoulder. It is doubtful if he survived. The other two were but slightly hurt. Billy had the heel of his boot battered, his gun shot to pieces, and received a wound in the hand. Jess. lost his hat. He said he knew when it was shot off his head, but where it went to he could not surmise.

CHAPTER VI.

Parts with Jess.—Segura Again—Dubbed "The Kid"—A Ride Rivaling that of Dick Turpin—The Gallant Gray—Jail Delivery Single Handed—Baffled Pursuers

After parting with the emigrants, whom they had so bravely rescued from the savages, Billy and Jess. changed their course and returned to the Rio Grande. Here they fell in with a party of young fellows, well known to Jesse, who urged them to join company and go over to the Rio Pecos, offering them employment which they guaranteed would prove remunerative. Among this party of "cow boys," were James McDaniels, William Morton, and Frank Baker, all well known from the Rio Grande to the Rio Pecos. Our two adventurers readily agreed to join fortunes with this party, and Jesse did so; but Billy received information, a day or two before they were ready to start, that his old partner Segura was in the vicinity of Isleta and San Elizario, Texas, and contemplated going up the Rio Grande to Mesilla and Las Cruces. Billy at once decided to await his coming, but promised his companions that he would surely meet them in a short time, either at Mesilla or in Lincoln County.

It was here, at Mesilla, and by Jim. McDaniels, that Billy was dubbed "The Kid," on account of his youthful appearance, and under this "*nom de guerre*" he was known during all his after eventful life, and by which appellation he will be known in the future pages of this history.

The Kid's new-found friends, with Jesse, left for Lincoln County, and he waited, impatiently, the arrival of Segura. He made frequent short trips from Mesilla, and, on his return from one of them, he led back his noted gray horse which carried him so gallantly in and out of many a "tight place" during the ensuing two years.

It was early in the fall of 1876 when The Kid made his famous trip of eighty-one miles in a little more than six hours, riding the gray the entire distance. The cause and necessity for this journey is explained as follows:

Segura had been detected, or suspected, of some lawless act at San Elizario, was arrested and locked up in the jail of that town. There was strong prejudice against him there, by citizens of his own native city, and threats of mob violence were whispered about. Segura, by promises of rich reward, secured the services of an intelligent Mexican boy and started him up the Rio Grande in search of The Kid, in whose cool judgment and dauntless courage he placed implicit reliance. He had received a communication from The Kid, and was about to join him when arrested.

Faithful to his employer, the messenger sought The Kid at Mesilla, Las Cruces, and vicinity, at last finding him at a ranch on the west side of the Rio Grande, about six miles north of Mesilla and nearly opposite the town of Doña Ana. The distance to San Elizario from this ranch was: To Mesilla, six miles, to Fletch. Jackson's (called the Cottonwoods), twenty-three miles, to El Paso, Texas, twenty-seven miles, and to San Elizario, twenty-five miles, footing up eighty-one miles. The ride, doubtless, exceeded that distance, as The Kid took a circuitous route to avoid observation, which he covered in a little more than six hours, as above stated.

He mounted on the willing gray, at about six o'clock in the evening, leaving the messenger to await his return.

He remarked to the boy that he would be on his way back, with Segura, by twelve o'clock that night. The boy was skeptic, but The Kid patted his horse's neck. "If I am a judge of horseflesh," said he, "this fellow will make the trip," and away he sped.

> "O swiftly can speed my dapple gray steed,
>   Which drinks of the Teviot clear;
> Ere break of day: the warrior 'gan say,
>   'Again will I be here.'"

Avoiding Mesilla, the horseman held down the west bank of the river, about eighteen miles to the little plaza of Chamberino, where, regardless of fords, he rushed into the ever treacherous current of the Rio Grande.

"Each wave was erected with tawny foam." More than once the muddy waters overwhelmed horse and rider. For thirty minutes or more, The Kid and his trusted gray battled with the angry waves, but skill, and strength, and pluck prevailed, horse and rider emerged, dripping, from the stream, full five hundred yards below the spot where they had braved the flood.

And now they rushed on, past the Cottonwood, past that pillar which marks the corner where join Mexico, New Mexico, and Texas, past Hart's Mills, until The Kid drew rein in front of Ben Dowell's saloon, in El Paso, then Franklin, Texas.

> "A moment now he slacked his speed,
> A moment breathed his panting steed."

It was now a quarter past ten o'clock, and the gray had covered fifty-six miles. The bold rider took time to swallow a glass of Peter Den's whiskey and feed his horse a handful of crackers. In ten minutes, or in less, he was again speeding on his way, with twenty-five miles between him and his captive friend.

About twelve o'clock, perhaps a few minutes past, one of the Mexicans who were guarding Segura at the lock-up in San Elizario was aroused by a hammering voice calling in choice Spanish to open up. "Quien es?" (Who's that?) inquired the guard.

"Turn out," replied The Kid. "We have two American prisoners here."

Down rattled the chain, and the guard stood in the doorway. The Kid caught him gently by the sleeve and drew him towards the corner of the building. As they walked, the shining barrel of a revolver dazzled the vision of the jailer, and he was notified in a low, steady, and distinct tone of voice that one note of alarm would be the signal for funeral preliminaries. The guard was convinced, and quickly yielded up his pistol and the keys. The Kid received the pistol, deliberately drew the cartridges, and threw it on top of the jail. He gave instructions to the jailer and followed him into the hall. The door of the room in which Segura was confined was quickly opened, and the occupant cautioned to silence. The Kid stood at the door, cocked revolver in hand, and, in low tones, conversed with Segura, occasionally addressing a stern mandate to the affrighted guard to hasten, as he bungled with the prisoner's irons.

All this was accomplished in the time it takes to relate it. With the assistance of Segura the two guards were speedily shackled together, fastened to a post, gagged, the prison doors locked, and the keys rested with the guard's revolver on top of the house. The Kid declared himself worn out with riding, mounted his old partner on the gray, then taking a swinging gait, which kept the horse in a lope, they soon left the San Elizario jail and its inmates far behind. Taking a well-known ford, they crossed the Rio Grande, and in a little more than an hour were sleeping at the ranch of a Mexican confederate. This friend hid the plucky horse on the bank of the river, mounted a mustang, and took the direction of San Elizario to watch the denouement, when the state of affairs should be revealed to the public.

Before daylight, the faithful friend stood again before his cabin with The Kid's horse and a fresh, hardy mustang, saddled and bridled. He aroused the sleepers. Quickly a cup of coffee, a tortilla, and a scrag of dried mutton were swallowed, and again, across the prairie, sped the fugitives.

Two hours later, a party of not less than thirty men, armed and mounted, rode up to the ranch. The proprietor, with many a malediction, in pure Castellano, launched against "gringos ladrones," related his tale of robbery and insult, how his best horse had been stolen, his wife insulted, and his house ransacked for plunder. He described the villains accurately, and put the pursuers on their trail. He saw them depart and returned sadly to his home, to mourn, in the bosom of his family, over the wickedness of the world, and to count a handful of coin which The Kid had dropped in making his hasty exit.

The pursuers followed the trail surely, but it only led them a wild goose chase across the prairie, a few miles, then making a detour, made straight for the bank of the Rio Grande again. It was plain to see where they entered the stream, but the baffled huntsmen never knew where they emerged.

The Kid and his companion reached the ranch where the Mexican boy awaited them about noon the next day. This messenger was rewarded with a handful of uncounted coin and dismissed.

And thus, from one locality after another, was The Kid banished by his bloody deeds and violations of law. Yet, not so utterly banished. It was his delight to drop down, occasionally, on some of his old haunts, in an unexpected hour, on his gallant gray, pistol in hand, jeer those officers of the law, whose boasts had slain him a hundred times, to watch their trembling limbs and pallid lips, as they blindly rushed to shelter.

"One instant's glance around he threw,
From saddle-bow his pistol drew,
Grimly determined was his look;
His charger with his spurs he struck,
All scattered backward as he came,
For all knew—"

And feared "Billy, The Kid." His look was hardly "grim," but through his insinuating smile, and from his blazing eyes, enough of "determination" and devilish daring gleamed to clear the streets, though twenty such officers were on duty.

CHAPTER VII.

A Wild Venture in the Guadalupe Mountains—The Mescalero Apaches Again—Bloody Work—The Loudest Call Yet—Scaling an Almost Perpendicular Precipice—Miraculous Escape

"He trusted to his sinewy hands,
And on the top unharmed he stands."

When The Kid again visited Mesilla, he found letters from Jesse Evans and his companions, urging him to join them on the Rio Pecos, near Seven Rivers without delay. They, however, warned him not to attempt the nearer, and, under ordinary circumstances, more practicable route, by the Guadalupe Mountains, as that country was full of Apache Indians, who always resented encroachments upon their domains. They advised him to follow the mail route, by Tularosa and the plaza of Lincoln. The very scent of dangerous adventure, and the prospect of an encounter with Indians, who were his mortal aversion, served as a spur to drive The Kid to his destination by the most perilous route. Segura used all his powers of persuasion to divert him from his hazardous undertaking, but in vain. As Segura could not be persuaded to accompany him, they parted again, and for the last time.

The Kid now sought a companion bold enough to brave the danger before him, and found one in a young fellow who was known as Tom O'Keefe. He was about The Kid's age, with nerve for almost any adventure. These two boys prepared themselves for the trip at Las Cruces.

The Kid left his gray in safe hands, to be sent on to him upon his order. Though the horse was fleet and long-winded, a common Mexican plug would wear him out in the mountains. So The Kid and O'Keefe procured two hardy mustangs, rode to El Paso, bought a Mexican mule, loaded him with provisions and blankets, and two seventeen-year-old lads started forth to traverse nearly two hundred miles of Indian country, which the oldest and bravest scouts were wont to avoid.

The second night in the mountains, they camped at the opening of a deep cañon. At daylight in the morning, The Kid started out prospecting. He climbed the cañon, and seeing some lofty peaks to the northwest, he labored in their direction, with the intention of scaling one of them to determine his bearings. He had told Tom he would return by noon. He was back in little more than an hour, and announced that he had struck an Indian trail not three hours old, that he was sure these Indians were making their way to water, not only from the lay of the country, but from the fact that they had poured water out on the ground along the trail.

"I'll not trouble these red-skins to follow me," said The Kid; "I shall just trail them awhile."

"Don't you think," said Tom, "it would be better to take our own trail, and follow that awhile?"

"No," replied The Kid. "Don't you see we have got to have water? It's close by. Those breech-clouts are going straight to it. I believe a little flare up with twenty or thirty of the sneaking curs would make me forget I was thirsty, while it lasted, and give water the flavor of wine after the brigazee was over."

"Can't we wait," said Tom, "until they leave the water?"

"O," replied The Kid, "we'll not urge any fight with them; but suppose they camp at the springs a week? They'll smell us out ten miles off. I'd rather find them than that they should find us. I am going to have water or blood, perhaps both."

They soon struck the Indians' fresh trail and followed it cautiously for an hour, or more, then they suddenly brought up against the bare face of a cliff. The trail was under their feet, leading right up to the rock; but, at its base, a ragged mass of loose stones were seen to be displaced, showing the route of the Indians turning short to the right, and, by following this, they discovered an opening, not more than three feet wide, surrounded and overhung with stunted shrubs and clambering vines.

The Kid dismounted and peered through this opening, but could see only a short distance, as his vision was obscured by curves in the pass. They took the back track a short distance, when, finding a tolerable place of concealment for their animals, they halted. The Kid took their only canteen and prepared to explore the dreaded pass. He told Tom that he should return on a run, and shouting to leave the mule, bring out the horses, and mount, ready to run; "and," said he, "if I bring water, don't fail to take the canteen from my hand, drink as you run, then throw the canteen away."

All Tom's arguments to dissuade The Kid from his purpose were useless. Said he: "I would rather die fighting than to perish from thirst, like a rat in a trap." Boldly, but cautiously, The Kid entered the dark and gloomy passage. Crouching low, he noiselessly followed its windings some one hundred yards, as he judged, then he suddenly came to an opening, about thirty feet wide, and stretching away towards the southwest, gradually narrowing until a curve hid its further course from his sight. The passage and opening were walled with rock, hundreds of feet high.

Grass and weeds were growing luxuriantly in this little amphitheatre, and a glance to the left discovered a bubbling mountain spring, gushing forth from a rocky crevice, bright, clear and sparkling.

Hugging the base of the cliff, creeping on hands and knees, The Kid, with canteen in readiness, approached the brink of a little basin of rock. The ground about was beaten by horses' hoofs, and water, recently splashed about the margin of the spring, evidenced that the reds had lately quitted the spot. Face and canteen were quickly plunged into the cool stream. The Kid drank long and deep, his canteen was overflowing, and stealthily he moved away. Entering the passage, he was congratulating himself on his good fortune, when suddenly a fearful Indian yell and a volley of musketry from, almost, directly over his head, on the right, dispelled his vision of safety. His signal cry rang out in answer, then, dashing his canteen in the faces of the Indians, who could only approach singly from the defile, he snatched his six-shooter from its scabbard, wheeled, and swiftly as any Mescalero of them all, plunged into the gorge he had just quitted, pursued by how many savages he did not know, and by yells and showers of lead.

Let us return for a moment to O'Keefe. He heard The Kid's dreaded shouts, and, simultaneously, the rattle of fire-arms and the blood-curdling war cry of the Indians. He followed The Kid's instructions so far as to bring the horses out to the trail, then the irresistible impulse of self-preservation overcame him and he mounted and fled as fast as the sinuous, rugged path would permit. The yells of the bloody Apaches, multiplied by a thousand echoes, seemed to strike upon his ears, not alone from his rear, but from the right of him, the left of him, the front of him, and as it resounded from peak to peak, he was persuaded that myriads of dusky devils were in pursuit, and from every direction.

Spying a cleft in the rocks, on his right, inaccessible to a horse, he threw himself from the saddle, gave the affrighted mustang a parting stroke, which sent him clattering down the steep declivity, then, on hands and knees, crawled into the chasm. Never casting a look behind, he crept on and up, higher and higher, until, as he reached a small level plateau, he thought he had surely attained the very summit of the mountains. The discharge of arms and savage shouts still fell faintly on his ears. Tremblingly he raised to his feet. His hands and limbs were scratched, bruised, and bleeding, and his clothing nearly stripped from his body. Faint with loss of blood, exertion, and thirst, he cast his blood-shot eyes over the surrounding crags and peaks. For some moments he could discern no sign of life, except here and there a huge bird, startled from his lofty perch by unwonted sounds, lazily circling over the scene of conflict beneath.

Tom's eyelids were drooping, and he was about to yield to an uncontrollable stupor, when his unsteady gaze was caught by a weird, to him incomprehensible, sight. Away off to the southeast, right on the face of a seemingly perpendicular mountainside, high up the ragged peak, as though swinging, without support, in mid-air, he descried a moving object, unlike beast or bird, yet rising slowly up, and higher up the dizzy cliff. His eye once arrested, gazing long and steadily, he could clearly discern that it was the figure of a man. Sometimes hidden by the stunted vegetation, cropping out from clefts of the rock, and sometimes standing erect, in bold relief, he still ascended—slowly, laboriously. Tom could also see masses of rock and earth, as they were dislodged by daring feet, and hear them, too, as they thundered down into the abyss below, awakening a thousand echoes from surrounding mountains.

It dawned, at last, upon O'Keefe's bewildered senses that this bold climber could be none other than The Kid, that he had essayed this fearfully perilous ascent as the only means of escape from the Indians. Again Tom's momentarily aroused intellects deserted him, and, utterly exhausted, he sank down upon the rock and slept profoundly.

Let us return to The Kid, whom we left in imminent peril. He had secured a copious draught of water, and felt its refreshing effect. He had left his Winchester with Tom, as he was preparing to run and not to fight. Thus, he had only his trusty six-shooter and a short dirk to make a fight against twenty well-armed savages thirsty for blood.

As The Kid darted into the narrow passage which led back to the spring, the Indians were but a few paces behind; but when they reached the opening, their prey was nowhere to be seen. Instinctively they sought his trail and quickly found it. They followed it for a few moments silently. The moments were precious ones to The Kid. The trail led them straight up to an apparently inaccessible cliff; they voluntarily raised their eyes, and there, as if sailing in open air, high above their heads, they descried their quarry. The Kid, however, quickly disappeared behind a friendly ledge, while such a yell of baffled rage went up as only an Apache can utter, and lead rained against the mountain side, cutting away the scant herbage and flattening against the resisting rock.

In an instant a half-dozen young braves were stripped for the pursuit. One, a lithe and sinewy young fellow, who appeared to possess the climbing qualities of the panther, quickly reached a point but a few feet beneath where The Kid had disappeared. For one instant an arm and hand projected from the concealing ledge, a flash, a report, and the bold climber poised a moment over the space beneath; then, with arms extended, a death-cry on his lips, he reeled and fell, backward, bounding from ledge to ledge, until he lay, a crushed and lifeless mass, at the feet of the band. The Kid made a feint, as if to leave his concealment, thus drawing the fire of the savages, but ere their guns were brought to bear on him, he darted back to shelter, again quickly appeared, and amidst yells of hate continued his ascent. Two or three desperate leaps from crag to crag, and he found another uncertain place of concealment. The pursuers, undaunted by the fate of their comrade, held steadily on their way. The Kid's body was now stretched forth from his hiding place in full sight, his gaze directed below, and amidst a shower of bullets his revolver again belched forth a stream of death-laden fire, and another Apache receives a dead-head ticket to the Happy Hunting Grounds. The inert body of this converted savage caught on a projecting ledge and hung over the chasm.

And now our hero seems to scorn concealment and bends all his energies towards mastering the ascent of the precipice, where not even an Apache dared to follow. As he several times paused to breathe, he leaned away out of the yawning gulf beneath, jeered his foes in Spanish, and fired wherever he saw a serape or a feather to shoot at. Bullets showered around him as he boldly but laboriously won his way, foot by foot. He seemed to bear a charmed life. Not a shot took effect on his person, but he was severely wounded in the face by a fragment of rock rent from the face of the cliff by a bullet.

The magic pen of Scott portrays the "frantic chase" of Bertram Risingham, in pursuit of the supposed spirit of Mortham, over "rock, wood and stream." The feats of the fabled Bertram, the pursuer, and the actual feats of the veritable The Kid, the pursued, bear strong comparison. Sings Scott:

"his frantic chase
Sidelong he returns, and now 'tis bent

Right up the rock's tall battlement,
Straining each sinew to ascend,
Foot, hand and knee, their aid must lend.

Now, to the oak's warped roots he clings,
Now trusts his weight to ivy strings;
Now, like the wild goat, must he dare
An unsupported leap in air;
Hid in the shrubby rain, course now,
You mark him by the crashing bough,
And by his corslet's sullen clank,
And by the stones spurned from the bank,
And by the hawk scared from her nest,
And ravens croaking o'er their guest,
Who deem his forfeit limbs shall pay
The tribute of his bold essay.

"See, he emerges! desperate now
All further course—Yon beetling brow,
In cragged nakedness sublime,
What heart or foot shall dare to climb?
It bears no tendril for his clasp,
Presents no angle to his grasp;
Sole stay his foot may rest upon,
Is yon earth-bedded jetting stone.
Balanced on such precarious prop,
He strains his grasp to reach the top.
Just as the dangerous stretch he makes,
By Heaven, his faithless foot stool shakes!
Beneath his tottering bulk it bends,
It sways, it loosens, it descends!
And downward holds its headlong way,
Crashing o'er rock and copsewood spray;
Loud thunders shake the echoing dell!
Fell it alone?—alone it fell.
Just on the very verge of fate,
The hardy Bertram's falling weight
He trusted to his sinewy hands,
And on the top unharmed he stands!"

More than once on that mountain side, like Bertram, The Kid trusted his whole weight to his "sinewy hands," and more than once did he dare "an unsupported leap in air." In after days he used to say that the nearest he ever came to having nightmare, was trying to repeat that journey in his dreams.

Safely The Kid reached the top of the peak. He felt no fear of pursuit from Indians, as he knew they had abandoned the perilous route himself had taken, and it would require days to make a detour so as to intercept him on the south. Yet his situation was forlorn, not to say desperate. Almost utterly exhausted from exertion, bruised, bleeding, footsore, famishing for food and water, yet sleep was what he most craved, and that blessing was accessible. Like O'Keefe, he sank down in a shady nook and wooed "balmy sleep, Nature's sweet restorer."

CHAPTER VIII.

The Kid Joins his Companions—"The Lincoln County War"—The Rights of Property a Myth—The Kid Takes a Change of Base, on Principle

We left The Kid at the end of the last chapter, sleeping peacefully on the top of one peak of the Guadalupe Mountains, and O'Keefe, also asleep, on a bench of another peak of the same range. The distance between them, air line, was not so far, but there was more than distance intervening. Cañons, precipices, crags, and brush to say nothing of a possible band of savages, burning with baffled hate and deadly revenge. "So near, and yet so far." They both awoke the next morning, as the sun appeared in the east. Each speculated on the fate of the other. The Kid made a straight break towards the rising sun, after reaching the valley beneath his last night's resting place, and reached the cow camps on the Rio Pecos in three days. He procured water at long intervals, but no food except wild berries during the whole trip. He had walked the entire distance and was pretty essentially used up when he reached the camps. After a few days rest, having informed himself how his entertainers stood as between the two factions in the Lincoln County War, he made himself known and was immediately armed, mounted, and accompanied to a stronghold of the Murphy-Dolan faction by one of the cattle-owners, where he again met Jesse Evans and his comrades, with whom he had parted on the Rio Grande.

The Kid was very anxious to learn the fate of O'Keefe, and induced two or three of the boys to accompany him again to Las Cruces, intending, should he hear no tidings of him there, to return by the Guadalupe route and try to hunt him up, or, failing in that, to "eat a few Indians," as he expressed it. He never deserted a friend. He had another errand at Las Cruces. His favorite gray was there, and he pined to bestride him once more.

Let us go back to O'Keefe in the wild passes of the mountains. Like The Kid, he had slept long and felt refreshed. But, less fortunate than his fellow, he had failed to get water the day previous, and was suffering intensely, not only from thirst but from hunger.

His first impulse was to place the greatest possible distance between himself and the scene of horror which had been enacted so recently; but his sufferings for lack of water were becoming acute. He felt a sort of delirium, and the impulse to return to the spring and procure water was irresistible. Yet he lingered in concealment, listening in terror and suffering untold agony, until night fell—the moon afforded a little light—and he found both the spring and the canteen. Hastily slaking his thirst and filling the canteen, he returned to the spot where he had left The Kid's horse and the pack-mule.

He found the dead body of the horse, pierced with balls, not a dozen yards from where he had last seen him, but there was no sign of the mule, and Tom addressed himself to the task of journeying, on foot, back to the settlements.

Throughout the night and long into the following day he plodded on. Like The Kid, he found a few green berries with which he "fed hunger." Near noon he ran into a deserted Indian camp where they had recently stopped to roast mescal. Poking about amongst the stones and earth around the pits, he found plenty of half-roasted refuse, which furnished him an ample feast and more than he cared to burden himself with for his after use on the journey.

In a few hours the wanderer reached the level prairie at the foot of the mountains in the south. His good luck had not deserted him yet. In the soft earth he espied the foot prints of his own horse which he had deserted. Night was coming on, but weary as he was, he followed the trail until darkness hid it from view. Just as he was about to seek a "soft place" on which to pass the night, he saw on his right, and a hundred yards distant, a moving object. To be brief, it was his own horse; he slept in his saddle blankets that night, and, in due time, made his way safely back to the Rio Grande.

The meeting, at Las Graces, between The Kid and O'Keefe was a surprise and a satisfaction. The Kid's efforts to induce Tom to join him in his Lincoln County enterprise were without avail. He had seen enough of that locality and did not hanker after a second interview with the Mescaleros.

"The Lincoln County War," in which The Kid was now about to take a part, had been brewing since the summer of 1876, and commenced in earnest in the spring of 1877. It continued for nearly two years, and the robberies and murders consequent thereon would fill a volume. The majority of these outrages were not committed by the principals or participants in the war proper, but the unsettled state of the country caused by these disturbances called the lawless element, horse and cattle thieves, footpads, murderers, escaped convicts, and outlaws from all the frontier states and territories; Lincoln and surrounding counties offered a rich and comparatively safe field for their nefarious operations.

It is not the intention, here, to discuss the merits of the embroglio—to censure or uphold either one faction or the other, but merely to detail such events of the war as the hero of these adventures took part in.

The principals in this difficulty were, on one side, John S. Chisum, called "The Cattle King of New Mexico," with Alex A. McSween and John H. Tunstall as important allies. On the other side were the firm of Murphy & Dolan, merchants at Lincoln, the county seat, and extensive cattle-owners, backed by nearly every small cattle-owner in the Pecos Valley. This latter faction was supported by Hon. T. B. Catron, United States attorney for the Territory, a resident and eminent lawyer of Santa Fe, and a considerable cattle-owner in the Valley.

John S. Chisum's herds ranged up and down the Rio Pecos, from Fort Sumner way below the line of Texas, a distance of over two hundred miles, and were estimated to number from 40,000 to 80,000 head of full-blood, graded, and Texas cattle. A. A. McSween was a successful lawyer at Lincoln, retained by Chisum, besides having other pecuniary interests with him. John H. Tunstall was an Englishman, who only came to this country in 1876. He had ample means at his command, and formed a co-partnership with McSween at Lincoln, the firm erecting two fine buildings and establishing a mercantile house and the "Lincoln County Bank," there. Tunstall was a liberal, public-spirited citizen, and seemed destined to become a valuable acquisition to the reliable business men of our country. He, also, in partnership with McSween, had invested considerably in cattle.

This bloody war originated about as follows: The smaller cattle-owners in Pecos Valley charged Chisum with monopolizing, as a right, all this vast range of grazing country—that his great avalanche of hoofs and horns engulfed and swept away their smaller herds, without hope of recovery or compensation—that the big serpent of this modern Moses, swallowed up the lesser serpents of these magicians. They maintained that at each "round-up" Chisum's vast herd carried with them hundreds of head of cattle belonging to others.

On Chisum's part he claimed that these smaller proprietors had combined together to round-up and drive away from the range—selling them at various military posts and elsewhere throughout the country—cattle which were his property and bearing his mark and brand under the system of reprisals. Collisions between the herders in the employ of the opposing factions were of frequent occurrence, and, as above stated, in the winter and spring of 1877 the war commenced in earnest. Robbery, murder, and bloody encounters ceased to excite either horror or wonder.

Under this state of affairs it was not so requisite that the employees of these stockmen should be experienced *vaqueros* as that they should possess courage and the will to fight the battles of their employers, even to the death. The reckless daring, unerring markmanship, and unrivalled horsemanship of The Kid rendered his services a priceless acquisition to the ranks of the faction which could secure them. As related, he was enlisted by McDaniels, Morton, and Baker, who were adherents to the Murphy-Dolan cause.

Throughout the summer and a portion of the fall of 1877, The Kid faithfully followed the fortunes of the party to which he had attached himself. His time was spent on the cattle-ranges of the Pecos Valley, and on the trail, with occasional visits to the plazas, where, with his companions, he indulged, without restraint, in such dissipations as the limited facilities of the little *tendejons* afforded. His encounters with those of the opposite party were frequent, and his dauntless courage and skill had won for him name and fame, which admiration, or fear, or both, forced his friends, as well as his enemies, to respect. No noteworthy event occurred during The Kid's adherence to the Murphy-Dolan faction, and he declared that all the uses of his life were "flat, stale, and unprofitable."

The Kid was not satisfied. Whether conscientious scruples oppressed his mind, whether he pined for a more exciting existence, or whether policy dictated his resolve, he determined to desert his employers, his companions, and the cause in which he was engaged and in which he had wrought yeoman's service. He met John H. Tunstall, a leading factor of the opposition. Whether The Kid sought this interview, or Tunstall sought him, or befell by chance is not known. At all events, our hero expressed to Tunstall his regret for the course he had pursued against him and offered him his future services. Tunstall immediately put him under wages and sent him to the Rio Feliz, where he had a herd of cattle.

The Kid rode back to camp and boldly announced to his whilom confederates that he was about to forsake them, and that when they should meet again,

> "Those hands, so fair together ranged,
> "Those hands, so frankly interchanged,"
> May dye "with gore the green."

Dark and lowering glances gleamed out from beneath contracted brows at this communication, and The Kid half-dreaded and half-hoped a bloody ending to the interview. Angry expostulation, eager argument, and impassioned entreaty all failed to shake his purpose. Perhaps the presence and intervention of his old and tried friend Jesse Evans stayed the threatened explosion. Argued Jesse: "Boys, we have slept, drank, feasted, starved, and fought cheek by jowl with The Kid; he has trusted himself alone amongst us, coming like a man to notify us of his intention; he didn't sneak off like a cur, and leave us to find out, when we heard the crack of his Winchester, that he was fighting against us. Let him go. Our time will come. We shall meet him again, perhaps in fair fight." Then, under his breath:—"and he'll make some of you brave fellows squeak." Silently and sullenly the party acquiesced, except Frank Baker, who insinuated in a surly tone that now was the time for the fight to come off.

"Yes, you d—d cowardly dog!" replied The Kid; "right now, when you are nine to one; but don't take me to be fast asleep because I look sleepy. Come you, Baker, as you are stinking for a fight; you never killed a man you did not shoot in the back; come and fight a man that's looking at you."

Red lightnings flashed from The Kid's eyes as he glared on cowering Baker, who answered not a word. With this banter on his lips, our hero slowly wheeled his horse and rode leisurely away, casting one long regretful glance at Jesse, with whom he was loth to part.

CHAPTER IX.

New Service—Apparent Reformation—A Firm Friend—Tunstall's Murder—The Kid's Rage—Revenge—Tunstall's Murderers Slain by The Kid—Baker Meets The Kid and Makes His Last Fight

After pledging allegiance to Tunstall, The Kid plodded along for some months in the monotonous groove fashioned for the "cow boy." In his bearing one would never detect the dare-devilism which had heretofore characterized him. He frequently came in contact with his employer and entertained for him strong friendship and deep respect, which was fully reciprocated by Tunstall. He was also ever a welcome guest at the residence of McSween. Both Tunstall and McSween were staunch friends to The Kid, and he was faithful to them to the last. His life passed on uneventfully. Deeds of violence and bloodshed were of frequent occurrence on the Pecos and in other portions of the country, but all was quiet on the Rio Feliz. The Kid had seemed to lose his taste for blood.

> "Fallen Child of Fortune, turn, redeem her favour here."

He was passive, industrious, and, seemingly, content. It was the lull before the storm.

In the month of February, 1878, William S. Morton (said to have had authority as deputy sheriff), with a posse of men composed of cow boys from the Rio Pecos, started out to attach some horses which Tunstall and McSween claimed. Tunstall was on the ground with some of his employees. On the approach of Morton and his party, Tunstall's men all deserted him—ran away. Morton afterwards claimed that Tunstall fired on him and his posse; at all events, Morton and party fired on Tunstall, killing both him and his horse. One Tom Hill, who was afterwards killed whilst robbing a sheep outfit, rode up as Tunstall was lying on his face, gasping, placed his rifle to the back of his head, fired, and scattered his brains over the ground.

This murder occurred on the 18th day of February, 1878. Before night The Kid was apprised of his friend's death. His rage was fearful. Breathing vengeance, he quitted his herd, mounted his horse, and from that day to the hour of his death his track was blazed with rapine and blood.

> "Pleasure, and ease, and sloth aside he flung,
> As burst the awakening Nazarite his band
> When 'gainst his treacherous foes he clenched his dreadful hand."

The Kid rode to Lincoln and sought McSween. Here he learned that R. M. Bruer had been sworn in as special constable, was armed with a warrant, and was about to start, with a posse, to arrest the murderers of Tunstall. The Kid joined this party, and they proceeded to the Rio Pecos.

On the 6th day of March, Bruer and his posse "jumped up" a party of five men below the lower crossing of Rio Penasco and about six miles from the Rio Pecos. They fled and the officer's party pursued. They separated, and The Kid, recognizing Morton and Baker in two of the fugitives who rode in company, took their trail and was followed by his companions. For fully five miles the desperate flight and pursuit was prolonged. The Kid's Winchester belched fire continually, and his followers were not idle; but distance and the motion of running horses disconcerted their aim, and the fugitives were unharmed. Suddenly, however, their horses stumbled, reeled, and fell, almost at the same instant. Perhaps they were wounded; no one paused to see. A friendly sink-hole in the prairie, close at hand, served the fleeing pair as a breastwork, from which they could have "stood off" twice the force behind them. And yet the pursuers had the best of it, as the pursued had but two alternatives—to surrender or starve.

After considerable parley, Morton said that if the posse would pledge their word and honor to conduct himself and his companion, Baker, to Lincoln in safety, they would surrender. The Kid strongly opposed giving this pledge. He believed that two of the murderers of Tunstall were in his power, and he thirsted for their blood. He was overruled, the pledge was given, the prisoners were disarmed and taken to Chisum's ranch. The Kid rode in the advance, and, as he mounted, was heard to mutter: "My time will come."

On the 9th day of March, 1878, the officer, with posse and prisoners, left Chisum's for Lincoln. The party numbered thirteen men. The two prisoners, special constable R. M. Bruer, J. G. Skurlock, Chas. Bowdre, The Kid, Henry Brown, Frank McNab, Fred Wayt, Sam Smith, Jim French, John Middleton and— McClosky. They stopped at Roswell, five miles from Chisum's, to give Morton the opportunity to mail a letter at the post-office there. This letter he registered to a cousin, Hon. H. H. Marshall, Richmond, Va. A copy of this letter is in the hands of the author, as well as a letter subsequently addressed to the postmaster by Marshall. Morton descended from the best blood of Virginia, and left many relatives and friends to mourn his loss.

Morton and the whole party were well known to the postmaster, M. A. Upson, and Morton requested him, should any important event transpire, to write to his cousin and inform him of the facts connected therewith. Upson asked him if he apprehended danger to himself on the trip. He replied that he did not, as the posse had pledged themselves to deliver them safely to the authorities at Lincoln, but, in case this pledge was violated, he wished his people to be informed. McClosky, of the officer's posse, was standing by and rejoined: "Billy, if harm comes to you two, they will have to kill me first."

The Kid had nothing to say. He appeared distrait and sullen, evidently "digesting the venom of his spleen." After a short stay the cortege went on their way. The prisoners were mounted on two inferior horses. This was the last ever seen of these two unfortunates, alive, except by the officer and his posse. It was nearly ten o'clock in the morning when they left the post-office. About four o'clock in the evening, Martin Chavez, of Picacho, arrived at Roswell from above, and reported that the trail of the party left the direct road to Lincoln, and turned off in the direction of *Agua Negra.* This was an unfrequented route to the base of Sierra de la Capitana, and the information at once settled all doubts in the minds of the hearers as to the fate of Morton and Baker.

On the 11th, Frank McNab, one of the posse, returned to Roswell and entered the post-office. Said Upson: "Hallo! McNab; I thought you were in Lincoln by this time. Any news?"

"Yes," replied he, "Morton killed McClosky, one of our men, made a break to escape, and we had to kill them."

"Where did Morton get weapons?" queried Upson.

"He snatched McClosky's pistol out of its scabbard, killed him with it, and ran, firing back as he went. We had to kill them, or some of us would have been hurt," explained McNab.

This tale was too attenuated. Listeners did not believe it. The truth of the matter, as narrated by The Kid, and in which rendering he was supported by several of his comrades, was as follows:

It had been resolved by two or three of the guards to murder Morton and Baker before they reached Lincoln. It has been stated by newspaper correspondents that The Kid killed McClosky. This report is false. He was not one of the conspirators, nor did he kill McClosky. He cursed Bruer, in no measured terms for giving a pledge of safety to the prisoners, but said, as it had been given, there was no way but to keep their word.

He further expressed his intention to kill them both, and said his time would come to fulfill his threat, but he would not murder an unarmed man.

McCloskey and Middleton constantly rode behind the prisoners, as if to protect them; the others brought up the rear, except The Kid and Bowdre, who were considerably in advance. About twenty or thirty miles from Roswell, near the Black Water Holes, McNab and Brown rode up to McClosky and Middleton. McNab placed his revolver to McClosky's head and said: "Your are the son-of-a-bitch that's got to die before harm can come to these fellows, are you?" and fired as he spoke. McClosky rolled from his horse a corpse. The terrified, unarmed prisoners fled as fast as their sorry horses could carry them, pursued by the whole party and a shower of harmless lead. At the sound of the first shot, The Kid wheeled his horse. All was confusion. He could not take in the situation. He heard fire-arms, and it flashed across his mind that, perhaps, the prisoners had, in some accountable manner, got possession of weapons. He saw his mortal enemies attempting to escape, and as he sank his spurs in his horse's sides, he shouted to them to halt. They held their course, with bullets whistling around them. A few bounds of the infuriated gray carried him to the front of the pursuers—twice only, his revolver spoke, and a life sped at each report. Thus died McClosky, and thus perished Morton and Baker. The Kid dismounted, turned Morton's face up to the sky, and gazed down on his old companion long and in silence.

> "Grief darkened on his rugged brow,
> Though half disguised with a frown."

He asked no questions, and the party rode on to Lincoln, except McNab, who returned to Chisum's ranch. They left the bodies where they fell. They were buried by some Mexican sheep-herders.

CHAPTER X.

Desperate Fight at the Indian Agency—One Man Stands Off a Dozen—Dies Fighting—Dick Bruer's Death—The Kid Calls for "Billy" Matthews—Killing of Sheriff Brady and Geo. Hindman in the Streets of Lincoln

Returning to Lincoln, The Kid attached himself to the fortunes of McSween, who was every day becoming more deeply involved in the events of the war. He was a peaceably disposed man, but the murder of his partner aroused all the belligerent passion within him. The Kid still adhered to Bruer's official posse, as hunger for vengeance was, by no means, satiated, and Bruer was still on the trail of Tunstall's murderers.

One of the actors in that tragedy was an ex-soldier named Roberts. The Kid heard that he could be found in the vicinity of the Mescalero Apache Indian Agency, at South Fork, some forty miles south of Lincoln. Roberts was a splendid shot, an experienced horseman, and as brave as skillful. Bruer and party were soon on their way to attempt his arrest. The Kid knew that he would never be taken alive by this party, with the fate of Morton and Baker, at their hands, so fresh in his memory; and this to The Kid, was a strong incentive to urge the expedition. It was life he wanted, not prisoners.

As the party approached the building from the east, Roberts came galloping up from the west. The Kid espied him, and bringing his Winchester to rest on his thigh, he spurred directly towards him as Bruer demanded a surrender. Roberts' only reply was to The Kid's movements. Like lightning his Winchester was at his shoulder and a ball sang past The Kid's ear. Quick as his foe, The Kid's aim was more accurate, and the ball went crashing through Roberts' body, inflicting a mortal wound. Hurt to the death, this brave fellow was not conquered, but lived to wreak deadly vengeance on the hunters. Amidst a shower of bullets he dismounted and took refuge in an out-house, from whence, whilst his brief life lasted, he dealt death with his rifle. He barricaded the door of his weak citadel with a mattress and some bed-clothing, which he found therein, and from this defense he fought his last fight. His bullets whistled about the places of concealment, where lurked his foes. Wherever a head, a leg, or an arm protruded, it was a target for his rifle. Charley Bowdre was severely wounded in the side, a belt of cartridges around his body saving his life. Here Dick Bruer met his death. Dr. Blazer's saw-mill is directly across the street from Roberts' hiding place. In front of the mill were lying numerous huge saw-boys. Unseen by Roberts, Bruer had crept behind these, to try and get a shot at him. But no sooner did Bruer raise his head to take an observation than the quick eye of Roberts detected him—but one of Bruer's eyes was exposed—it was enough—a bullet from a Winchester found entrance there, and Bruer rolled over dead behind the boy.

The brave fellow's time was short, but to his last gasp his eye was strained to catch sight of another target for his aim, and he died with his trusty rifle in his grasp.

To The Kid, the killing of Roberts was neither cause for exultation, nor "one for grief." He had further bloody work to do. He swore he would not rest nor stay his murderous hand so long as one of Tunstall's slayers lived.

"For he was fierce as brave, and pitiless as strong."

Bruer dead, the command of the squad, by common consent, was conferred upon The Kid. He had little use for the position, however, as throwing around his deeds the protection of law, which he held in disdain. What he wanted was two or three "free riders" who, without fear or compunction, would take their lives in their hands and follow where he led.

On their return to Lincoln, the posse was disbanded, but most of those composing it joined fortunes with The Kid as their accepted leader. With emissaries riding over the country in every direction, he bided his time and opportunity. He spent most of his time in Lincoln and frequently met adherents of the other faction, which meetings were ever the signal for an affray. J. B. Matthews, well known throughout the Territory as "Billy" Matthews, held The Kid in mortal aversion. He was not with the posse who killed Tunstall, but denounced, in no measured terms, the killers of Morton, Baker, and Roberts. He was an intimate friend of popular Jimmy Dolan of the firm of Murphy & Dolan, and a strong supporter of their cause. "Billy" was brave as any red-handed killer of them all. He was in Lincoln plaza on the 28th day of March, and, by chance, unarmed. He came suddenly face to face with The Kid, who immediately "cut down" on him with his Winchester. "Billy" darted into a doorway, which The Kid shot into slivers about his head. Matthews had his revenge, though, as will hereafter appear.

At this time William Brady was sheriff of Lincoln County. Major Brady was an excellent citizen and a brave and honest man. He was a good officer, too, and endeavored to do his duty with impartiality. The objections made against Sheriff Brady were that he was strongly prejudiced in favor of the Murphy-Dolan faction—those gentlemen being his warm personal friends, and that he was lax in the discharge of his duty through fear of giving offence to one party or the other. Yet the citizens of New Mexico will unite in rendering honor to the memory of an honest, conscientious, kind-hearted gentleman.

Sheriff Brady held warrants for The Kid and his associates, charging them with the murders of Morton, Baker, and Roberts. The Kid and his accomplices had evaded arrest by dodging Brady on the plaza and standing guard in the field. They resolved to end this necessity for vigilance, and by a crime which would disgrace the record of an Apache. The Kid was a monomaniac on the subject of revenge for the death of Tunstall. No deed so dark and damning but he would achieve it to sweep obstacles from the path which led to its accomplishment. Brady with his writs barred the way, and his fate was sealed.

On the 1st day of April, 1878, Sheriff Brady, accompanied by George Hindman and J. B. Matthews, started from Murphy & Dolan's store, Lincoln, to go to the court house, and there announce that no court would be held at the stated April term. In those days of anarchy a man was seldom seen in the plaza or streets of Lincoln without a gun on his shoulder. The sheriff and his attendants each bore a rifle. Tunstall & McSween's store stood about halfway between the two above named points. In the rear of the Tunstall & McSween building is a corral, the east side of which projects beyond the house and commands a view of the street, where the sheriff must pass. The Kid and his companions had cut grooves in the top of the adobe wall in which to rest their guns. As the sheriff came in sight a volley of bullets were poured upon them from the corral, and Brady and Hindman fell, whilst Matthews took shelter behind some old houses on the south side of the street. Brady was killed outright, being riddled with balls. Hindman was mortally wounded, but lived a few moments.

Ike Stockton, who was for so long a terror in Rio Arriba County, this Territory, and in Southern Colorado, and who was recently killed at Durango, kept a saloon in Lincoln plaza at the time the above recited event occurred, and was supposed to be a secret ally of The Kid and gang. He was a witness to the killing of Brady, and, at this moment approached the fallen men. Hindman called faintly for water. The Rio Bonito was close at hand, Stockton brought water to the wounded man in his hat. As he raised his head he discovered Matthews in his concealment. At this moment The Kid and his fellows leaped the corral wall and approached with the expressed intention of taking possession of the arms of Brady and Hindman. Ike knew that as soon as they came in view of Matthews, he would fire on them, and he was equally sure that were he to divulge Matthews presence, he would, himself, become a target. So he "fenced" a little, trying to persuade The Kid that he had not better disturb the arms, or to defer it a while. The Kid was, however, determined, and as he stooped and raised Brady's gun from the ground, a ball from Matthews' rifle dashed it from his hand and plowed a furrow through his side, inflicting a painful though not dangerous wound. For once The Kid was baffled. To approach Matthews' defense was to court death, and it was equally dangerous to persevere in his attempt to possess himself with Brady and Hindman's arms. Discretion prevailed and the party retired to the house of McSween. Hindman lived but a few moments.

This murder was a most dastardly crime on the part of The Kid, and lost him many friends who had, theretofore, excused and screened him.

CHAPTER XI.

Jesse Evans Again—The Kid and Jesse—Whilom Friends, Now Mortal Foes—Reminiscences—Bloodless Encounter—Tom O. Foliard

The Kid and his desperate gang were now outlawed in Lincoln, yet they haunted the plaza by stealth and always found a sure and safe place of concealment at McSween's. The laws were not administered, and they often dared to enter the plaza in broad day, defying their enemies and entertained by their friends.

For some space Lincoln County had no sheriff. Few were bold enough to attempt the duties of the office. At length, George W. Peppin consented to receive a temporary appointment. He appointed, in his turn, a score of deputies, and during his tenure of office, robbery, murder, arson, and every crime in the calendar united and held high carnival in their midst. The Kid was not idle. Wherever a bold heart, cool judgment, skillful hand, or reckless spirit was required in the interests of his faction, The Kid was in the van.

San Patricio, a small Mexican plaza on the Rio Ruidoso, some seven miles from Lincoln by a trail across the mountain, was a favorite resort for The Kid and his band. Most of the Mexicans there were friendly to him, and kept him well informed as to any movement which might jeopardize his liberty.

Jose Miguel Sedillo, a faithful ally of The Kid, brought him information, one day in June about daylight, that Jesse Evans with a party from below were prowling about, probably with the intention of stealing a bunch of horses belonging to Chisum and McSween, and which were in charge of The Kid and party.

Without waiting for breakfast, The Kid started with five men, all who were with him at that time. They were Charley Bowdre, Henry Brown, J. G. Skurlock, John Middleton, and Tom O. Foliard. This latter was a young Texan, bold and unscrupulous, who followed the fortunes of The Kid from the day they first met, literally to the death. At this time he had only been with the gang a few days.

Taking Brown with him, The Kid ascended a ridge on the west of the Ruidoso, and followed it up, towards the Bruer ranch, where he had left the horses. He sent Bowdre, in charge of the other three, with instructions to follow the river up on the east bank.

After riding some three miles The Kid heard firing in the direction where Bowdre and his men should be. The shots were scattering, as though a skirmish was in progress. He dismounted and sent Brown on to circle a hill on the left, whilst himself led his gray down the steep declivity towards the river and road and in the direction of the shooting. With much difficulty he reached the foot of the mountain, crossed the river, and was laboriously climbing a steep ascent on the east when the clatter of a single horse's feet arrested his attention, and, in a moment he descried Brown, through a gap of the hills, riding furiously towards the north, and, at that moment a fusillade of fire-arms saluted his ears. He mounted and then came a most wonderful ride of less than a mile; it was not remarkable for speed, but the wonder is how he made it at all. Through crevices of rock it would seem a coyote could scarce creep, over ragged precipices, through brush, cactus, and zacaton, he made his devious, headlong way, until, leaving the spur of hills he had with such difficulty traversed, another similar elevation lay in front of him, between the two a gorge some half mile across; and, at the foot of the opposite hill, the scene of conflict was in view. Jesse, with a band of eight men had attacked Bowdre's party; they were fighting and skirmishing amongst the rocks and undergrowth at the foothills, and were so mixed, confused, and hidden, that The Kid could scarce distinguish friends from foes. He spied Bowdre, however, in the hands of the enemy, among whom he recognized Jess., and, with one of his well-known war cries, to cheer his friends, he dashed madly through the gorge.

Bowdre's relation of previous events shows how Evans and men attacked him about two miles from the hills. Having an inferior force, he made a run for the foot-hills and took a stand there amongst the rock and brush. Several shots were fired during the chase. Evans made a detour of the hill to avoid the range of Bowdre's guns, and the skirmish commenced. Bowdre became separated from his men. He saw Brown as he rode to the rescue and sought ambush on the east of the hill. Evans also saw Brown, and sent a shower of lead after him, which was the volley that reached the ears of The Kid and brought him to the scene. Thinking to join Brown, who had not recognized him, Bowdre broke from cover on a run, but fell into the hands of Jesse and four of his men. He was powerless against numbers, and his only hope was to stand Evans off until assistance arrived. How he prayed for the appearance of The Kid as he shot anxious glances around. No shot was fired. Evans and party covered him with their revolvers, and Jesse's merry blue eyes danced with boyish glee, albeit a little devil lurked about the corners, as he bantered his prisoner:

"Where's your pard, Charley? I expected to meet him this morning. I'm hungry and thought I'd flay and roast The Kid for breakfast. We all want to hear him bleat."

Bowdre choked back the retort which rose to his lips. He was dismounted and his gun taken from the scabbard, where he had replaced it when surprised, but his captors made no motion to relieve him of his revolver. Bowdre stood with his hand resting on his horse's haunch. Three of Evans' men were dismounted, and two of their horses stood heads and tails, each bridle rein thrown over the other's saddle-horn. At this moment it was that The Kid's well-known yell rang out like the cry of a panther. The Evans crowd seemed paralyzed, and Bowdre remarked: "There comes your breakfast, Jess." All gazed wonderingly at the apparition of a gray horse, saddled and bridled, dashing across the valley, with no semblance of a rider save a leg thrown across the saddle and a head and arm protruding from beneath the horse's neck, but, at the end of this arm the barrel of a pistol glistened in the sun-light. Quicker than it can be told, there scarce seemed space to breathe 'till

> "Fast as shaft can fly,
> —his nostrils spread"

The gray dashed among the amazed gazers. The Kid's voice rang out: "Mount, Charley, mount." He straightened himself in the saddle and drew rein, but before he could check his headlong speed, the powerful gray had breasted the two horses which were hitched together, threw them heavily and one mounted man lost his seat, and fell beneath his horse. Triumph in his eye, Bowdre had seized his gun, unnoticed, and mounted, ranging himself beside The Kid.

> —"This -friend,
> O'er gasping heroes, rolling steeds,
> And snatched me from my fate."

This meeting was a sight not soon to be forgotten by those who witnessed it. These two young beardless desperadoes, neither of them yet twenty-one years of age—boyish in appearance, but experienced in crime—of nearly equal size, each had earned a reputation for desperate daring by desperate deeds, which had made their names a terror wherever they were known. They had slept together on the prairies, by camp fires, in Mexican pueblos, and on the mountain tops; they had fought the bloody Mescaleros and Chiricahuas side by side; they had shared their last dollar and their last chunk of dried deer meat, and had been partners in many other reckless and less creditable adventures, since their earliest boyhood.

No one would have thought, from their smiling faces, that these two were mortal foes. Their attitudes were seemingly careless and unconstrained, as they sat their chafing horses, each with a revolver, at full-cock, in his right hand, resting on his thigh. Though their eyes twinkled with seeming mirth, they were on the alert. Not for an instant did each take his eye from the other's face. As their restless horses champed the bit, advanced, retreated, or wheeled, that steady gaze was never averted. It seemed their horses understood the situation and were eager for the strife.

> "Their very coursers seemed to know
> That each was the other's mortal foe."

And thus, for a moment, they gazed. There was a little sternness in The Kid's eye, despite its inevitable smile. Jesse, at length, laughingly broke the silence.

"Well, Billy, this is a hell of a way to introduce yourself to a private picnic party. What do you want anyhow?"

"How are you, Jess.?" answered The Kid. "It's a long time since we met. Come over to Miguel Sedillo's and take breakfast with me; I've been wanting to have a talk with you for a long time, but I'm powerful hungry."

"I, too, have been wanting to see you, but not exactly in this shape," responded Jess. "I understood you are hunting the men who killed that Englishman, and I wanted to say to you that neither I nor any of my men were there. You know if I was I would not deny it to you nor any other man."

"I know you wasn't there, Jess.," replied The Kid. "If you had been, the ball would have been opened without words."

"Well, then," asked Jess., "what do you jump us up in this style for? Why you'd scare a fellow half to death that didn't know you as well as I do."

"O, ask your prisoner here, Charley," said The Kid, "he'll tell you all about it. You won't go to breakfast with me then? Well, I'm gone. One word, Jess., before I go. There's a party from Seven Rivers lurking about here; they are badly stuck after a bunch of horses which I have been in charge of. The horses are right over the hills there, at Bruer's old ranch. If you meet that crowd, please say to them that they are welcome to the horses, but I shall be there when they receive them, and shall insist that they take Old Gray and some other horses along, as well as me and a few choice friends. Come, put up your pistol, Jess., and rest your hand."

With these words The Kid slowly raised his pistol-hand from his thigh, and Jesse as deliberately raised his. The dancing eyes of Jesse were fixed on The Kid, and the darker, pleasant, yet a little sterner eyes of The Kid held Jesse's intently. Simultaneously the muzzles of their pistols were lowered, neither for an instant pointing in the direction of the other, then, with the spontaneous movement of trained soldiers, were dropped into their scabbards. As they raised their hands and rested them on the horns of their saddles, seven breasts heaved a sigh of relief.

"I have some more men scattered about here," remarked Jesse.

"And so have I," replied The Kid. "Now, Jesse., you ride down the arroyo," pointing east, "and I will ride to the top of the hills," pointing west. "I'll get my men together in a moment, and I suppose you can herd yours. No treachery, Jess. If I hear a shot, I shall know which side it comes from. Old Gray does not care in which direction he carries me, and he can run."

With these words, The Kid reined his horse towards the Rio Ruidoso, and without turning his head, rode leisurely away. Bowdre sat a moment and watched Evans, whose eyes followed The Kid. Jess., at last, wheeled, his horse, ejaculated: "By G—d, he's a cool one," called to his followers and dashed down the arroyo. Bowdre rejoined The Kid, and in twenty minutes the party of six were reunited and were trotting merrily, with sharpened appetites, to breakfast.

Thus ended this bloodless encounter. It was incomprehensible to their followers that these two leaders could meet without bloodshed; but, per chance, the memory of old times came over them and curbed their bold spirits.

"Yet, be it known, had bugles blown,
Or sign of war been seen,"

* * * *

"The merry shout—
    Had sunk in war-cries wild and wide."

Had one act of violence been proffered, by either of the leaders, they would have fought it out to the bloody, fatal end.

"And scorned, amid the reeling strife,

To yield a step for death or life."

CHAPTER XII.

Recruiting for Bloody Work—The Desperate Fight in Lincoln—The Kid Trapped—The Burning of McSween's Residence—Fearful Holocaust—Pluck to the Last—Death of McSween—The Kid Fights His Way through Twenty Assailants from the Burning Building—Escape

During all this time Sheriff Peppin was not idle, but could do little towards restoring peace in the distracted county. In selecting his deputies, he had chosen some brave and reliable business men, upon whom he could depend. Among these was Marion Turner, of the firm of Turner and Jones, merchants at Roswell. Turner had been for years, off and on, in the employ of Chisum, by whom he was trusted, and who valued his services highly. He had been a staunch adherent of Chisum at the commencement of his struggle and up to May, 1878, when he seceded, for what he probably deemed sufficient cause, and became his old employer's bitterest enemy. Turner had control of the sheriff's operations in the valley of the Rio Pecos, and soon raised a posse of between thirty and forty men, composed principally of cattle-owners and cow boys, few of whom knew the taste of fear.

Turner's headquarters were at Roswell, where the posse was encamped. The Kid with fourteen men visited Chisum's ranch, five miles from Roswell, early in July. Turner with his force went there with the intention of ousting him from his stronghold. He found this impracticable, as the houses were built with a view to defense against Indians, and a band of fourteen determined men could hold it against an army–barring artillery. Consequently Turner relinquished his attempt on the ranch, but kept spies constantly on the alert.

One morning Turner received information that The Kid had left his quarters and started up the Pecos towards Fort Sumner. He had several warrants against The Kid for murder, and he now swore to either arrest him, kill him, or die in the attempt. With his full force he took the trail. After riding some twenty miles he pronounced this movement of The Kid's to be a blind, and turning west, he left the trail and took a short, straight-out to Lincoln. The result proved his sound judgment, as The Kid and band were there, safely barricaded in the elegant and spacious residence of McSween, prepared to stand a siege and defend their position to the last. Sheriff Peppin with a few recruits joined Turner at the "Big House," as it was called, of Murphy and Dolan, a short distance from McSween's. Turner, however, was the ruling genius of the enterprise. For three days spasmodic firing was kept up from both sides, but no harm was done.

On the morning of July 19th, 1878, Turner expressed his intention of going to the house of McSween and demanding the surrender of The Kid and others against whom he held warrants. This project was denounced as foolhardy, and it was predicted that he would be shot down before he got within speaking distance. Nothing daunted, he persisted in his design and called for volunteers to accompany him. His partner, John A. Jones, than whom a braver man never lived in New Mexico, at once proffered to attend him, and his example was followed by eight or ten others.

The advancing party saw the port-holes which pierced the sides of the building, and, to their surprise, they were allowed to walk up to the walls and ensconce themselves between these openings without being hailed, or receiving a hint that their presence was suspected by those within. The explanation of this circumstance was that the besieged were at that moment holding a council of war in a room in the rear, where the whole garrison was assembled. The result of this discussion was, The Kid had sworn that he would never be taken alive; his ruling spirit had swayed the more timid, and it was resolved to drive off the assailants, or die at their posts. McSween appeared to be inert, expressing no opinion, or desire. As they returned to their posts, they were astonished to find the front yard occupied by their foes. The Kid hailed the intruders, when Turner promptly notified him that he held warrants for the arrest of Wm. H. Bonney, and others of his companions, amongst them Alex A. McSween.

The Kid replied:—"We, too, have warrants for you and all your gang, which we will serve on you, hot, from the muzzles of our guns." In short, The Kid and all his confederates refused to make terms, and Turner retired in safety. Not so, however, his attendants. Their position, once gained, they did not propose to relinquish. And now the fight commenced in earnest.

At this juncture, Lieut. Col. Dudley, of the Ninth Cavalry, arrived from Fort Stanton, nine miles distant, with one company of infantry and one of artillery. Planting his cannon in a depression of the road, between the belligerent parties, he proclaimed that he would turn his guns loose on the first of the two who fired over the heads of his command. Yet the fight went on, and the big guns were silent.

Turner was confident, and said he would have The Kid out of there if he had to burn the house over his head.

The Kid, on his part, was sanguine—he said he could stand the besiegers off, and was as gay as if he were at a wedding. Both knew that the struggle must be a bloody one, and neither anticipated an easy victory.

"Now closed is the gin, and the prey within,

> By the rood of Lanercost!
> But he that would win the war-wolfs skin,
> May rue him of his boast."

Turner's men took possession of all the surrounding buildings, from which and the McSween mansion desultory firing was kept up. Doors, windows, and other woodwork, were slivered by flying bullets, and earth flew from adobe walls. This fusillade from the besiegers was aimed to cover the operations of those allies within the yard, who were laboring to fire the building—working kindlings under door and window sills and wherever wood-work was exposed. A portion of The Kid's party had gained the roof, and from behind the parapets, harassed the foe. Turner sent a dozen men to the hills which overlook the plaza, and their heavy, long-range guns soon dislodged them. A magnificent piano in one of the front rooms was hit several times by these marksmen in the hill-tops, and at each stroke sent forth discordant sounds. This circumstance elicited from a Lamy, N. M., correspondent of the N. Y. *Sun*, the following:

> "During the fight Mrs. McSween encouraged her wild garrison by playing inspiring airs on her piano, and singing rousing battle songs, until the besieging party, getting the range of the piano from the sound, shot it to pieces with their heavy rifles."

The truth is Mrs. McSween and three lady friends, left the house before the fight commenced. It is also true that she requested permission to return for some purpose, the firing ceased—she went bravely in—returned almost immediately, and the firing was resumed.

About noon the flames burst forth from the front doors and windows, and the fate of the building was sealed. All efforts of the inmates to extinguish them were fruitless, and the assailants shouted their joy. Soon the whole front of the house was deserted by its defenders, and Jack Long having procured a little coal oil, less than a gallon, made his way into a room not yet on fire, carefully saturated the furniture with the oil, fired it, and made his escape. This "little dab" of coal oil got the Lamy correspondent off again: "On the third day of the skirmish Turner had the house fired by throwing buckets full of blazing coal oil into it and over it." Doesn't it seem that "blazing buckets full of coal oil" would be disagreeable to handle? An adobe building burns very slowly, and this was a large one, containing eleven rooms. Yet the flames were slowly and surely driving the inmates back. The besiegers called on them to surrender every few minutes. The only reply was curses and defiance.

And now, as night sets in the defenders have but one room, a kitchen at the back of the house, that is tenable, and this would furnish shelter but a short time. The question of surrender was discussed and vetoed by The Kid with [scorn]. Bloody, half naked, begrimed with smoke and dust, his reckless spirit was untamed. Fiercely he threw himself in the doorway, the only means of escape, and swore that he would brain and drag back into the burning building the first that made a motion to pass that door. "Hold," said he, "until the fire breaks through upon us, then all as one man, break through this door, take the underbrush on the Rio Bonito, and from there to the hills. We'll have an even chance with them in the bottom." This *ipse dixit* settled it. The Rio Bonito was not more than fifty yards from the back of the house.

And now one affrighted Mexican, unheeding The Kid's threat, precipitated the bloody *finale*. He called out to stop shooting and they would surrender. A blow from The Kid's revolver, and the presumptuous fellow lay bruised and senseless on the floor. The Kid had not time to execute all his threat. So soon as the Mexican's voice was heard on the outside, the firing ceased. Robert W. Beckwith, a cattle owner of Seven Rivers, with John Jones passed round the corner of the main building in full view of the kitchen doorway. No sooner did Beckwith appear than a shot from the house inflicted a wound on his hand. He saw The Kid and McSween in the door, and shouting "McSween! McSween," opened fire on them. The Kid shot but once, and Beckwith fell dead, the ball entering near the eye. The Kid called to "come on," and leaping over Beckwith's prostrate body, pistol in hand, he fought his way through a score of enemies, step by step he fought, until reaching the brink of the river he plunged across, and was hid from sight by weeds and brush. He was followed by all his band who had life and strength to flee, and several of those left a bloody trail behind. McSween less fortunate than The Kid, fell dead in the yard, refusing to surrender or to flee. He was pierced with nine bullets. Tom O. Foliard, the new recruit, was the last one who left the yard, and showed his pluck by stopping to pick up a friend, Morris. Discovering that he was dead, he dropped him, and amidst a shower of lead made his escape unharmed.

It was now ten o'clock at night. The fight for the present, was ended, the building was in ashes, there were seven mutilated corpses lying about, and several on both sides nursed desperate wounds.

Turner's party lost but one man killed, besides Beckwith. The Kid's party had killed McSween, Harvey Morris, and three Mexicans. Turner's party numbered about forty men, and The Kid's nineteen, aside from McSween.

CHAPTER XIII.

More Blood—Kills Bernstein—Threats against Chisum—Horse Stealing—The Big Bluffer Bluffed—Trip to the Pan Handle of Texas—In Jail at Lincoln—Escape—The Kid and Jesse Evans Again

After the disastrous events, detailed in the last chapter, The Kid gathered together such of his gang as were fit for duty and took to the mountains south of Lincoln. From thence they made frequent raids, stealing horses and mules from the vicinity of Dowlin's Mill, the Indian agency, Tularosa, and the Pecos Valley, varying the monotony by occasionally taking in a few ponies from the Mescaleros. They became bold in their operations, approaching the agency without fear.

On the 5th day of August, 1878, they rode up in full sight of the agency, and were coolly appropriating some horses, when the bookkeeper, named Bernstein, mounted on a horse and said he would go and stop them. He was warned of his danger by persons who knew The Kid and gang, but, unheeding, he rode boldly up and commanded them to desist. The only reply was from The Kid's Winchester, and poor Bernstein answered for his temerity with his life. This gentleman was a Jew, well known in the Territory. He had been in the employ of Spiegelberg Bros. and Murphy & Dolan previous to his connection with the agency, and was an excellent business man and accomplished gentleman.

Sheriff Peppin, with his cohorts, had retired from active service after the bloody nineteenth of July, and law was a dead letter in the county. Immediately after the killing of Bernstein, The Kid, accompanied by Foliard, Fred Wayt, Middleton, and Brown, went to Fort Sumner, San Miguel County, eighty-one miles north of Roswell on the Rio Pecos. Here they established a rendezvous, to which they clung to the last chapter of this history. Bowdre and Skurlock were both married. Their Mexican wives were devoted to them and followed their fortunes faithfully. These two, Bowdre and Skurlock, remained in Lincoln County for a time, but, in the absence of their chief, avoided publicity. The Kid and friends, in the meantime, applied themselves industriously to the pursuit of pleasures. They worshipped, religiously, at the shrines of Bacchus and Venus, but only for a brief space. They had arrived at Sumner on the 18th day of August. About the first of September, this party of five started for Lincoln, for the purpose of assisting Bowdre and Skurlock to remove their families to Sumner. This feat was accomplished without any adventure of moment.

On the tenth of September, The Kid, with three of his party, again left Sumner for Lincoln County—this time bent on plunder. Chas. Fritz, Esq., living on his ranch eight miles east of Lincoln, on the Rio Bonito, was a steady friend of Murphy & Dolan's during all the troubles, and his hospitable dwelling was always open to their friends. Hence, The Kid and his ilk bore him no good will. They made a descent on his ranch and got away with eighteen or twenty horses, most of them valuable ones. With their booty they returned to Sumner and secreted the stock near by.

There was at Fort Sumner at this time, a buffalo-hunter who had just returned from the plains named John Long, or John Mont, or John Longmont. He was a six-footer, a splendid shot, and coveted the reputation of a "bad man." He was a boisterous bully.

A day or two after The Kid returned from his raid on Fritz, Long, in a drunken frenzy, was shooting his revolver promiscuously up and down the street of Sumner, and the terrified citizens had mostly retired from sight. The Kid issued from a store and, to avoid the bullets, sprang behind a tree-box. Here was an opportunity for Long, to whom The Kid was unknown, to exhibit his magnanimity.

"Come out, buddy," said he; "don't be afraid, I won't hurt you."

"The h—l you won't!" replied The Kid. "There's no danger of your hurting anybody, unless you do it accidentally. They say you always kill your men by accident."

This retort hit Long hard, as he had killed a man at Fort Griffin, Texas, a short time previously, and saved himself from a furious mob by pleading that it was an accident. He eyed The Kid viciously and queried:

"Where are you from, buddy?"

"I'm from every place on earth but this," responded The Kid, and Long walked sullenly away.

On the following day Long, with several companions, was indulging in a big drunk in a little *tendejon* kept by a Jew. Long was, as usual, the biggest, the loudest, and the drunkenest of the crowd. The Kid entered, in company with young Charley Paine, and the two passed to the back of the store. Long hailed them:

"Where are you going? you d—d little son-of-a-b—h," said he.

The Kid wheeled quickly and walked up to him, with something glistening in his eye which wise men are wont to "let their wisdom fear," and said:

"Who did you address that remark to, sir?"

"O!" answered Long, with a sickly smile, "I was just joking with that other fellow."

"Be very careful," replied The Kid, "how you joke fellows in whose company I happen to be. You will notice that I am the 'littlest' of the two. I am too stupid to understand or appreciate your style of jokes, and if you ever drop another one that hits the ground as close to me as that last, I'll crack your crust; do you understand?"

Long made no reply. He was completely cowed. The Kid gazed sternly at him a moment, and walked carelessly away. The big fighter annoyed him no more. He was killed shortly afterwards at a ranch on the plains by a Mexican named Trujillo.

The Kid remained at Sumner but a few days, when he, Foliard, Bowdre, Wayt, Brown, and Middleton, took the horses stolen from Fritz and started up the Rio Pecos with the intention of adding to their herd before they drove them away. They raided Grzelachowski's ranch, at Alamo Gordo, and other ranches at Juan de

Dios and the vicinity of Puerta de Luna, forty miles north of Fort Sumner, and increased their stock of animals to thirty-five or forty head.

Pretty well "heeled," they took a course nearly due east, and in the direction of the Pan Handle of Texas. At Theackey's ranch Bowdre sold out his interest in the stolen stock to his companions, and rejoined Skurlock, at Sumner, where he was employed by Peter Maxwell, to herd cattle. The Kid with the remaining four went on to Atascosa, on the Canadian, leaving Fort Bascom on their left and passing through the plaza of Trujillo.

After the outlaws were gone, the citizens about Puerta de Luna aroused themselves, and one Fred Rothe, then a resident of Las Colonias, now of Anton Chico, raised a party of eight or ten Mexicans, rode to Fort Sumner to enlist more men, failed to increase his force, followed the trail of the stolen stock to Hubbell Springs, about twenty-five miles, got a good look at both thieves and plunder, but, not being on speaking terms with The Kid, and too modest to accost him, and without firing a shot, returned to the river.

The Kid and his band quickly disposed of their ill-gotten plunder, and almost as quickly exhausted the proceeds at monte table and saloons. There was little show to make a winning on the Canadian and the party discussed future movements. Middleton, Wayt, and Brown were tired of the life of danger and privation they had been leading for some months past, and announced their unalterable intention to turn their backs on New Mexico and its bloody scenes forever. They urged The Kid and Foliard to accompany them, and predicted their tragic end, should they return. All arguments failed. Neither party could be persuaded to abandon their designs, and they parted company forever. Middleton, Brown, nor Wayt have never been seen in New Mexico since.

The Kid and Foliard returned to Fort Sumner and joined Bowdre and Skurlock. Bowdre continued in the employ of Maxwell, but was interested in all the illegal traffic of his friend. The Kid must have some object upon which to concentrate his energies. Tunstall, during his life had been, not only his friend, but his banker. He was dead, and amply revenged. Then McSween had supplied the place of Tunstall in his friendship and interest. McSween, also, was dead. There was left but John S. Chisum, of the trio, in whose service he had worked, fought, and killed. But Chisum failed to respond to his petitions for assistance—or remuneration, as The Kid chose to term it—and he conceived for Chisum a mortal hatred, which he tried to flatter himself was justified by his refusal to countenance him in his lawless career, but which was, doubtless, merely feigned as an excuse to plunder Chisum's vast herds of cattle and horses. So upon his return from the Canadian, his energies were all enlisted in cattle "speculations," Chisum, per force, furnishing the capital.

In December, 1878, The Kid and Foliard again visited Lincoln. George Kimbreel had been elected sheriff in November, and held warrants for both of them. They were arrested and placed in the old jail, from whence they easily made their escape and returned to Fort Sumner, where they continued their cattle raids, living in clover; and The Kid by his pleasing manners and open-handed generosity made himself almost universally popular.

Lincoln, with a properly exercised authority, would have been a dangerous locality for The Kid, but he flickered like a moth around the flame. To his daring spirit it was fun to ride through the plaza and salute citizens and officers with a cheerful *buenos dias.*

In the month of February, 1879, The Kid again met Jesse Evans, and in the plaza, at Lincoln. James J. Dolan was about delivering a herd of cattle to the agents of Thomas B. Catron. Dolan had reached a point near Lincoln with his herd, and visited the plaza with two of his employees—Jesse Evans and Wm. Campbell. That night the three, in company with Edgar A. Waltz, agent and brother-in-law of Catron, and J. B. Matthews, met The Kid and Foliard in the street. The meeting was by appointment, and after a few sharp words, ended in a reconciliation—all pledging themselves to bury the hatchet, and cease their, now, causeless strife. At the commencement of the interviews, Jesse said to The Kid: "Billy, I ought to kill you for murdering Bob. Beckwith." The Kid replied: "You can't start your lead pump any too quick to suit me, Jess. I have a hundred causes to kill you." Dolan and Matthews interfered as peacemakers, and the threatened row was quelled.

The parties, so reconciled, adjourned to a saloon and drowned old animosities in whisky. Late in the night a lawyer named Chapman arrived in the plaza from Las Vegas. He had been employed by Mrs. McSween to settle up the estate of her deceased husband. It was charged that Chapman was busily engaged in blowing the embers of a dead struggle, and he had made enemies. As he was passing The Kid and party, who had just issued from the saloon, Campbell, who was chuck-full of bad whiskey and fight, accosted him and told him he wanted to see him dance. Chapman replied indignantly. But few words passed when Campbell shot him dead. The Kid and Jesse were thus witnesses to one killing in which they did not take a hand. The misfortune of this affair was that two innocent parties were arrested, with the guilty one, for this crime. Dolan and Matthews were indicted, tried, and triumphantly acquitted. Campbell was arrested, placed in the guard-house at Fort Stanton, made his escape and fled the country. The Kid and Jess. parted that night never to meet again.

CHAPTER XIV.

Nabbed Again—Handwriting on the Wall—Another Escape—Defying the Sheriff—Kills a Texas Desperado—The Kid as a Financier—Promiscuous Horse and Cattle Stealing

Leaving Lincoln after his interview with Evans, The Kid returned to Fort Sumner, and, securing some new recruits to his service, he inaugurated a system of plunder which baffled all resistance; and a stock-owner's only course to secure immunity from loss, was to conciliate The Kid and court his friendship. The property of those he claimed as friends he held sacred.

There was an attraction in the very danger which attended The Kid's presence in Lincoln. Again in March, 1879, he, with Foliard, took a trip to that plaza. Upon this occasion they made a showing to comply with the law, and on their arrival, laid away their guns and revolvers. They were again arrested on the old warrants, and placed under guard in the house of Don Juan Patron, and handcuffed; but otherwise their confinement was not irksome. They were guarded by Deputy Sheriff T. B. Longworth, and The Kid had pledged his word to him that he would make no attempt to escape. Longworth knew him well and trusted him. They did not betray this trust until they were again placed in jail. They led a gay life at the house of Patron. Plenty to eat and drink, the best of cigars, and a game of poker with any one, friend or stranger, who chanced to visit them. The Kid was cheerful and seemingly contented. His hand was small and his wrist large. When a friend entered, he would advance, slip his hand from the irons, stretch it out to shake hands and remark:—"I don't wish to disgrace you, sir"; or, "you don't get a chance to steal my jewelry, old fellow."

On the 21st day of March, 1879, Longworth received orders to place the two prisoners in jail—a horribly dismal hole, unfit for a dog-kennel. The Kid said:—"Tom, I've sworn I would never go inside that hole again alive."

"I don't see," said Tom, "how either you or I can help it. I don't want to put you there, I don't want to put any one there; but that's orders, and I have nothing to do but to obey. You don't want to make trouble for me?"

The Kid walked gloomily up to the jail door and, stopping, said to Longworth:—"Tom, I'm going in here because I won't have any trouble with you, but I'd give all I've got if the son-of-a-b—h that gave the order was in your boots."

He passed into the hall, his cell was pointed out to him, the door of unpainted pine was standing open, he took a pencil from his pocket and wrote on it:

> William Bonney was incarcerated first time, December, 22, 1878; Second time, March, 21, 1879, and hope I never will be again.

W. H. Bonney.

This inscription still stands, and was copied by the author in August, 1881.

It is suspected that the sheriff knew the prisoners' stay in jail would be short, and he was tired of feeding them. At all events they left when they got ready, and The Kid prowled about the plaza for two or three weeks, frequently passing up and down in broad day, with a Winchester in his hand, cursing the sheriff to his heart's content.

In April they returned to Fort Sumner, and resumed depredations on loose stock, and followed the business industriously throughout the summer and fall. In October of 1879, The Kid, with Foliard, Bowdre, Skurlock, and two Mexicans, rounded up and drove away from Bosque Grande, twenty-eight miles north of Roswell, one hundred and eighteen head of cattle, the property of Chisum. They drove them to Yerby's ranch—in his absence—branded them, and turned them loose on the range. This ranch is north of Sumner. They said that Chisum owed them $600 each for services rendered during the war. They afterwards drove these cattle to Grzelachowski's ranch, at Alamo Gordo, and sold them to Colorado beef-buyers, telling them that they were employed in settling up Chisum's business. Chisum followed the cattle up, recovered them, and drove them back to his range—but The Kid had the money, and displayed a rare genius as a financier in its disbursement. Out of about $800 he generously gave Bowdre $30, "because he had a family;" Foliard was a disgrace to the band on account of shabby boots—he got a new pair as his share; the Mexicans got "the shake," and there was yet Skurlock to dispose of. He got four or five different parties to go to Skurlock and warn him of the intended arrest of the gang by officers of Lincoln County, which so scared him up that he borrowed fifty pounds of flour from Pete Maxwell, gathered together his family and household goods and skipped the country. Thus is Doc. Skurlock, henceforth, lost to this history. Out of $800 he got fifty pounds of flour which still stands charged, P. & L., on Pete Maxwell's books. When asked what he would do with his share, The Kid said he would endow an insane asylum, if he could catch Doc. Skurlock.

In January, 1880, a fellow named Joe Grant, arrived at Fort Sumner, and was straightaway cheek by jowl with The Kid and his companions. It afterwards transpired that Grant had heard a good deal of The Kid and aspired to win a reputation as a "Holy Terror," as he termed it, by killing the New Mexico desperado. That he had killed his man, and was a "bad one," there is no doubt. He disclosed a good deal of his disposition, if not his intention, one day in Sumner, by remarking: "I like to pick these fighters and lay them out on their own dung hill. They say The Kid is a bad citizen, but I am his loadin' any jump in the road." The Kid heard this, but kept his own counsel, drinking and carousing with Grant every day. Whilst Grant was swaggering and boasting, The Kid was in his usual jovial humor, but no movement of his companion escaped his wary eye.

James Chisum, brother of John S., with three men, had been to Cañon Cueva, near Juan de Dios, north of Fort Sumner, and there recovered a bunch of cattle which had been stolen from their range, it was said, by The Kid. He returned as far as Sumner, arriving there one day about the middle of January, and camped within a mile of the plaza. His party were young Herbert, Jack Finan, and William Hutchison, known on the range as "Buffalo Bill." The Kid, Barney Mason, and Charley Thomas rode out to Chisum's camp and demanded to look through his herd for the XIX brand. They did so, but found none.

The Kid then, good-naturedly insisted that Chisum and his men should go to Bob. Hargrove's saloon and take a drink. There they found Joe Grant, viciously drunk. As the party entered, he snatched a fine ivory-handled pistol from Finan's scabbard, and put his own in place of it. The Kid had his eye on him, and remarking "That's a beauty, Joe," took the pistol from his hand and revolved the chambers. It was his design to extract some of the cartridges, but he found only three in it, and deftly whirling the chambers until the next action would be a failure, he returned it to Grant, who flourished it about and at last said to The Kid:

"Pard, I'll kill a man quicker'n you will for the whisky."

"What do you want to kill anybody for?" answered The Kid. "Put up your pistol and let's drink."

During this conversation, Grant had passed behind the counter, and was knocking decanters and glasses about with the pistol. Thus, with the counter between him and the crowd, and revolver in hand, it seemed he had "the drop" on any one in the room whom he might want. The Kid remarked:

"Let me help you break up house-keeping, Pard," and drawing his pistol, also went to knocking the glassware about. Grant continued:—

"I want to kill John Chisum, any how, the d—d old——," and he eyed James Chisum with a wicked glare.

"You've got the wrong pig by the ear, Joe," said The Kid; "That's not John Chisum."

"That's a lie," shouted Grant; "I know better"; and, turning his pistol full on The Kid, who was smiling sarcastically, he pulled the trigger, but the empty chamber refused to respond; with an oath he again raised the hammer, when a ball from The Kid's revolver crashed through his brains, and he fell behind the counter. The Kid threw the shell from his pistol and said:

"Unfortunate fool; I've been there too often to let a fellow of your calibre overhaul my baggage. Wonder if he's a specimen of Texas desperadoes."

Some one remarked that, perhaps Joe was not killed, and he had better watch out for him.

"No fear," replied The Kid. "The corpse is there, sure, ready for the undertaker."

He sauntered off, unconcernedly, gave orders to a Mexican for the burial, then calling to "Buffalo Bill," he said;—

"Bill, stay right with your horse and watch your gun. You had better get your party away soon as possible. There are some petty-larceny thieves in the plaza who may take a notion to give you a game. I don't like one of the Chisum family, and d—d few of their friends; but this crowd is here by my invitation, and I won't see it handicapped."

The Chisum party got away with the loss of one gun, stolen from their wagon during their absence at the saloon.

Shortly after the killing of Grant, The Kid made a trip below, remaining for some weeks in the vicinity of Roswell. Verando, three miles from that place, was his headquarters. He was "flush" and spent money freely. The Chisum ranch was but about seven miles from Verando, and those who knew him best suspected that The Kid harbored the intention of waylaying Chisum and urging a fight with him. He kept himself pretty full of whisky, and upon one occasion, at Verando, he was sitting in front of the saloon where a covey of snow-birds were hopping about. He drew his revolver and remarked:—"Suppose, boys, old John Chisum was a pretty little bird, which he is not, and suppose that pretty little bird sitting in that straw was him; now if I was to shoot that little bird, and hit him anywhere except in the head, it would be murder;" and with the words, he fired. A bystander picked up the dead bird, and its head was shot off. "No murder!" cried The Kid. "Let's give old John another chance," and another bird's head disappeared. He killed several in this manner, until at last he hit one in the breast. "I've murdered old John at last," said he, "let's go and take a drink."

CHAPTER XV.

Various Stock Raids—Depredations at and near White Oaks—Fight with Sheriff's Posse—Daring Venture in White Oaks—Barricaded and Surrounded—Murder of Carlyle—Another Escape

No event of importance attended The Kid's visit below, and, on his return to Fort Sumner, he enlisted Billy Wilson, Mose Dedrick, Pas. Chavez, Iginio Salazar, and Senor Mora in an enterprise which had for its object the acquisition of Indian ponies. They went to the

Mescalero Apache Indian reservation and stole forty-eight head from those Indians. The Kid must have become avaricious, as it is said he appropriated thirty head of this lot to his own use and benefit. They were traded off all up and down the Rio Pecos.

The expedition above mentioned was made from Bosque Grande in February, 1880. In May The Kid, Bowdre, Pruett, and one other accomplice, name unknown, left Fort Sumner and went in an easterly direction. Near Los Portales, they stole a bunch of fifty-four head of beef cattle, belonging to cattle-owners on the Canadian in the Pan Handle of Texas. These they drove to White Oaks and sold to Thomas Cooper for $10 per head.

They returned to Fort Sumner some time in June with a bunch of horses stolen by them in the vicinity of White Oaks.

In July, they stole a bunch of cattle from John Newcomb at *Agua Azul* (Blue Water), about fifteen miles from Lincoln at the base of Sierra de la Capitana, branded and turned them loose on the range.

During the summer they made various successful raids. They drove off ten head of work-steers, property of a Mexican of Fort Sumner, and sold them together with twenty head more to John Singer, of Las Vegas. The Mexican followed Singer, overtook him near Las Vegas, and recovered his cattle.

About the 15th of November, The Kid, Foliard, Tom Pickett, and Buck Edwards stole eight head of fine horses from the ranch of A. Grzelachowski, at Alamo Gordo, and started in the direction of White Oaks with them. They traded four of them to Jim Greathouse, turned two out on the Cienega Macha, and kept two for their own use. Of these latter two, one was subsequently shot under The Kid and the other captured at Coyote Springs. The owner eventually recovered all except the one killed.

On the night of the 22d of November, 1880, an attempt was made by unknown parties to get away with some horses of J. B. Bell's, who lived in the southwestern portion of the town of White Oaks. On the following morning, the rumor was rife and it was reported to the officers that The Kid and gang were in camp at Blake's Saw Mill, near town. On this information, Deputy Sheriff William H. Hudgens summoned a posse, comprising the following citizens: Geo. Neil, John N. Hudgens, John Longworth, James Carlyle, Jas. S. Redmond, J. P. Eaker, J. W. Bell, and William Stone. This party lost no time in visiting the outlaws' camp, but found it deserted. They, however, struck the trail and followed it in the direction of Coyote Springs. About five miles from White Oaks, the posse met Mose Dedrick and W. J. Lamper riding in the direction of town. These men were known to be friends of The Kid and his band, and it was also known that they had left White Oaks that morning about the same time with the officer's posse. Hudgens suspected that they had been to a rendezvous of The Kid's, to give information and convey provisions. On this suspicion they were arrested.

The posse rode on to the vicinity of Coyote Springs, when they were fired on from a concealed, temporary camp of the outlaws, and a horse ridden by John Hudgens, the property of O'Neil, was killed. The fire was quickly returned. The Kid's horse fell dead under him, and after brief delay the outlaws fled. On reaching the camp, Hudgens found a fine saddle, said to be the property of The Kid, beside the dead body of the horse. They also found an overcoat, known to have been worn in White Oaks that morning by Mose Dedrick, and another known to have been the property of Sam Dedrick, brother to Mose. The Kid was known to be without an overcoat, and his friend Sam had doubtless supplied the "much felt want;" at all events, the coat was worn frequently in his presence thereafter by one of the captors, but Dedrick did not claim it. Besides the spoils above named, the sheriff's posse found a considerable quantity of canned goods and provisions together with a pair of saddle-bags containing useful dry goods, all of which were known to have been purchased at White Oaks that morning.

Deputy Sheriff Hudgens then returned to town with his party, arriving there about dark. The Kid's crowd became separated during the melee, Cook and Edwards not answering to roll-call. The Kid waited until the other party were well out of sight, when he, too, took the road to White Oaks, and the pursued became the pursuers. They committed no depredation in the town, but appeared to seek concealment. They rode to the stables and corral of West & Dedrick, where they all remained except The Kid, who went to the main street of the town.

A gentleman who knew The Kid well and was known by him, was standing just inside the door of a club-room when The Kid entered with his broad-brimmed hat drawn down over his eyes. This gentleman was about to address him, when a quick, warning glance and an ejaculation—"*Chicto! compadre*" (hush! pardner)—stayed his salutation. The Kid kept in the background, but bore himself with as much *nonchalance* as if he were an hourly visitor there. If anyone else observed him it was not his enemy, or he feared the consequences of giving the alarm, as fully one-half of Hudgen's posse were in the room, and they were brave men. On the first intimation of his presence, a bloody carnival would have been inaugurated, wherein more than one man would have bit the dust; and, though The Kid seemed to bear a charmed life, his escape would have been little less than a miracle. There is little doubt but he went to the club-room with murder in his heart, and the instrument on his person, but against whom his vengeance was directed can only be surmised. Some unknown person's absence from that room saved his life, as no fear of danger would have stayed The Kid's hand had he found the victim he sought. More than one heart throbbed tumultuously, and more than one cheek paled when, the following morning, it was known that The Kid had been in their midst.

On the following night, November 23 (and The Kid's birthday), he, with his companions, rode boldly into White Oaks about nine o'clock, and, seeing Jim Redmond standing in front of Will Hudgen's saloon, fired on him. The night was dark, the shelter of buildings was handy, and no one was hurt. They rode out of town, and, on the outskirts, came upon Jimmy Carlyle and J. N. Bell, whom Hudgens had left on guard. These fired on the outlaws, but with no visible effect.

On the 24th and 25th of November, the prisoners, Mose Dedrick and Lamper, were brought before Probate Judge Jas. A. Tomlinson for examination. Lamper was discharged and Dedrick was placed under bonds to secure his appearance before the district court. He skipped the country and the bond was forfeited.

Another posse was raised by Constable T. B. Longworth on the evening of November 23rd. This party consisted of Constable Longworth, Deputy Sheriff William H. Hudgens, John N. Hudgens, James Watts, John Mosby, James Brent, J. P. Langston, Ed. Bonnell, W. G. Dorsey, J. W. Bell, J. P. Eaker, Charles Kelley, and James Carlyle. They left White Oaks that evening, took the Las Vegas road and proceeded to the ranch of Greathouse & Kuck, about forty miles distant. Here, from what they believed to be sure information, they expected to find The Kid and his band.

They arrived at their destination about three o'clock on the morning of the 27th and erected four breastworks at available points within easy gun-shot of the house, behind which they awaited daylight.

The first visible movement at the house was the appearance of the German cook, named Steck, who was brought in by Eaker and Brent, trembling with fear. He soon told all he knew. The Kid and his gang were hived.

Will Hudgens wrote a note to The Kid, demanding his surrender, and sent it to the house by Steck. He soon returned accompanied by Greathouse, and bearing The Kid's reply:—"You can only take me a corpse." Hudgens told Greathouse he wanted The Kid, Dave Rudabaugh, and Billy Wilson. To this Greathouse replied:— "If you want them, go and take them." Hudgens then sent word to Billy Wilson, requesting him to come out and talk to him, pledging himself that after the conversation, if he refused to surrender, he should be allowed to return to the house unharmed. Wilson declined leaving the house, but he wanted to see Jimmy Carlyle, that perhaps he might surrender, and in his turn pledged his word that Carlyle should not be detained nor hurt. It is generally believed that Wilson would have surrendered, but that he was restrained by The Kid and Rudabaugh, as there was no charge of capital crime against him then—but this would not be said of him when the sun set that day.

Hudgens refused to allow Carlyle to go to the house when Greathouse said:—"Let him go, there will no harm come to him. I, myself will remain here as a hostage, and if he is hurt, let my life answer for the treachery." Still Hudgens withheld his consent, until Carlyle himself announced his determination to interview Wilson, resisted all arguments to dissuade him from his purpose, disarmed himself, and entered the—to him—fatal stronghold.

Greathouse remained with the officer's party. The hours passed away, and anxious friends awaited the appearance of Carlyle in vain. It was discovered that the outlaws were well supplied with whiskey in the house, and conjectures as to the effect that might have on the result of the interview were exchanged.

About two o'clock, p.m., those on the outside were startled by a crash from the house—a window was shattered—Carlyle appeared at the opening—leaped out and made a rush for the barricades—a sharp rattle of firearms from within, and Carlyle fell dead within ten feet of the window. One word to the memory of poor Jimmy. He was a young blacksmith who had been in the Territory a little more than a year, but in that short time had made hundreds of friends, and not one enemy. He was honest, generous, merry-hearted, quick-witted, and intelligent. His bloody murder excited horror and indignation, and many who had viewed the career of The Kid with some degree of charity now held him in unqualified execration as the murderer of an exceptionally good man and useful citizen.

Constable Longworth had been dispatched to White Oaks for reinforcements and provisions. The posse had been without food and water for more than twenty-four hours, and had suffered intensely from cold and exposure. They did not deem it practicable to attempt to hold out until Longworth's arrival, so returned as far as Hocradle's ranch, about fifteen miles from White Oaks, and twenty-five from Greathouse and Kuck's. They held Greathouse by no legal process. He had assumed his position, as they believed, in good faith, and he was released.

The Kid and party reconnoitered carefully, convinced themselves that their enemies had retired, and left under the cover of night. They were all on foot, and made direct for the ranch of a confederate, a few miles distant, got breakfast and left hurriedly in the direction of Anton Chico, twenty-five miles below Las Vegas on the Rio Pecos. John Hurley, a deputy sheriff, had raised a posse at Lincoln to reinforce Longworth. He met Longworth's party at Hocradle's ranch, got what information he could, went to the ranch of Greathouse, took the outlaw's trail to the ranch of their confederate, where they had taken breakfast, found the birds flown, but burned the ranch and thus wiping out one rendezvous of the gang. This posse then returned to Lincoln.

Jim Greathouse did not remain long at his ranch after The Kid and party left. He was next seen at Anton Chico, and it is strongly suspected that he supplied the outlaws with horses there. They were seen near Anton Chico one evening on foot—Greathouse was in the plaza—the next morning they were mounted and took breakfast at Lane's mail station, fifteen miles east of there. They lost no time at the station, taking a southerly direction to Las Cañaditas. Their number was reduced to three—The Kid, Dave Rudabaugh, and Billy Wilson. At Las Cañaditas they were joined by Tom O. Foliard, Charley Bowdre, and Tom Pickett, thus doubling their force.

CHAPTER XVI.

Counterfeit Money—United States Detective—Business Men Confederates of The Kid—On Track of the Outlaws—One Arrested—Webb and Davis

In the month of October, 1880, just previous to the events narrated in the last chapter, the author of this history first became personally and actively engaged in the task of pursuing and assisting to bring to justice The Kid, and others of his ilk, in an official capacity. The reader will perceive how awkward it would appear to speak of myself in the third person, so at the risk of being deemed egotistical, I shall use the first person in the future pages of this work.

In October, Azariah F. Wild, a detective in the employ of the Treasury Department, hailing from New Orleans, La., visited New Mexico to glean some information in regard to the circulation of counterfeit money, some of which had certainly been passed in Lincoln County. Mr. Wild sent for me to go to Lincoln and confer with and assist him in working up these cases. I met him there, and in the course of our interview, I suggested that it would be policy to employ a reliable man to join the gang and ferret out the facts. Wild at once adopted the plan, giving me authority to act in the matter according to my judgment.

I returned to my home, near Roswell, and immediately sent to Fort Sumner for Barney Mason, whom I had tried and knew I could trust. Mason came to me at once, and before I could name the matter to him, he told me that he had stopped at Bosque Grande, twenty-eight miles above, at the ranch of Dan Dedrick, and that Dan had read to him a letter from W. H. West, partner of his brother Sam. Dedrick, in the stable business at White Oaks. The gist of the letter was that West had $30,000 in counterfeit greenbacks, that his plan was to take this money to Mexico, there buy cattle with it, and drive them back across the line. He wanted to secure the services of a reliable assistant whose business would be to accompany him, West, to Mexico, make sham purchases of the cattle as fast as they were bought, receiving bills of sale therefor, so that, in case of detection, the stock would be found in legal possession of an apparently innocent party;—and the latter suggested Barney Mason as just the man to assume the role of scape-goat in these nefarious traffickings.

Mason was considerably surprised when he knew that this was the very business on which I had sent for him. Accompanied by Mason, I returned to Lincoln, and Wild, after giving Mason full instructions, and finding that he comprehended them, employed him, at a stipulated salary, *per diem* and expenses, to go to White Oaks and fall in with any proposition which might be made to him by West, Dedrick, or any other parties.

Mason left Lincoln for White Oaks, November 20. The night he arrived there, he went to West and Dedrick's stable to look after his horse. Let it be understood that there are three brothers of the Dedrick's—Dan. who lived at Bosque Grande at this time, but is now a partner of Sam at Socorro, is the oldest. Sam at that time was a partner of West, at White Oaks, and Mose, the youngest, who was floating promiscuously over the country, stealing horses, mules, and cattle, is now on the wing, having jumped a bail bond.

As Mason entered West and Dedrick's corral, he met The Kid, Dave Rudabaugh, and Billy Wilson. Rudabaugh had killed a jailer at Las Vegas in 1879 whilst attempting to liberate a friend named Webb. He was on the dodge, and had associated himself with The Kid. Billy Wilson had sold some White Oaks property to W. H. West and received in payment $400 in counterfeit money. This he had spent (as is alleged), and flourished around promiscuously. He, also, was on the dodge. There was no graver charge at that time against Wilson; but the murder of Carlyle, a few days subsequent, as related in the last chapter, renders him liable to indictment for complicity in that crime.

Mason was well known to the three outlaws, and had always been on friendly terms with them. They addressed him in their usual good-natured manner, The Kid asking him what brought him there. Mason's reply intimated that a chance to "take in" a band of horses near by was the cause of his presence. The Kid "smelled a rat," had an interview with his friends and Dedrick, and wanted to kill Mason right there, of which design Mason was ignorant until afterwards. Dedrick vetoed the plans at once—he knew it would be dangerous to him and to his business.

J. W. Bell, afterwards my deputy, was known by Mason to be a friend of mine, so he sought him and advised him of the presence of The Kid and party at the corral. Bell raised a posse of citizens and then went alone to the stable. He interviewed West, who assured him that those he sought were not there. He then inquired about their horses, and West declared that they had no horses there. That statement was false, as West and Dedrick slipped the horses out to the gang during the night.

Mason remained at White Oaks several days, but, owing to the intense excitement caused by the presence of The Kid, and his pursuit by the citizens, he did not deem it a fitting time to broach the subject of his visit to West. I had told him to be sure and see me before he started to Mexico and to come to Roswell in a few days at all hazards. He reached my house on the 25th.

In the meantime I was daily hearing of the depredations of The Kid and gang in the vicinity of White Oaks. I had heard that they were afoot, and guessed that they would go to Dan Dedrick, at Bosque Grande, for horses. I sent word to my neighbors, requesting them to meet me at Roswell, five miles from my house, after dark. I imparted my plans to Mason and he volunteered to accompany me. We left home in the evening. When near Roswell we saw a man riding one horse and leading another. He was going south, in the direction of Chisum's ranch. We went on to Roswell, and found that this wayfarer had avoided that place, and concluded he was dodging. Knowing that The Kid's party had become separated, we thought he might be a straggler from that band, trying to get out of the country.

Mason knew all The Kid's party, so taking him with me, we pursued and caught up with the fugitive near Chisum's ranch. Mason at once recognized him as Cook, who had fled from the fight at Coyote Springs. We disarmed him, took him back to Roswell, and put him in irons. Capt. J. C. Lea had Cook in charge for some three or four weeks, then sent him to jail at Lincoln, from whence he made his escape.

My neighbors had responded to my call, and, about nine o'clock that night, I started up the Rio Pecos with a posse, consisting of the following named citizens:—Messrs. Lawton, Mitchell, Mason, Cook, Whetstone, Wildy, Mc-Kinney, Phillips, Hudson, Olinger, Roberts, and Alberding. At daybreak we surrounded Dedrick's ranch, at Bosque Grande twenty-eight miles north of Roswell. Here we found two escaped prisoners from the Las Vegas jail. One was Webb, who had been sentenced to hang for the killing of a man named Killeher, at Las Vegas, and had taken an appeal. The other was Davis, who was awaiting trial for stealing mules. These two had made their escape, in company with three others, two of whom had been killed whilst resisting re-arrest, and the other had been returned to the jail at Las Vegas. We found no other person whom we wanted; so, causing Webb and Davis to fall into ranks, we proceeded up the Rio Pecos, arriving at Fort Sumner about daylight the morning of the 27th of November. Here I received a letter from Capt. Lea, detailing further depredations of The Kid and band about White Oaks, the killing of Carlyle, etc. I gained some further information from a buckboard driver, and determined to leave the two prisoners, Webb and Davis, under guard at Sumner, and pursue the outlaws. I went to A. H. Smith, a citizen of Sumner, and made inquiries. He assured me that The Kid and his two companions had not yet returned from the vicinity of White Oaks, but that Foliard, Bowdre, and Pickett were at Cañaditas, about twenty miles, north of east, from Fort Sumner, where Bowdre was in the employ of T. G. Yerby.

Stopping at Fort Sumner only long enough to get breakfast, I left four of my men in charge of the prisoners and, with the balance, started for Las Cañaditas. Olinger and myself were both commissioned as deputy United States marshals, and held United States warrants for The Kid and Bowdre for the killing of Roberts on an Indian reservation.

CHAPTER XVII.

Chase on the Prairie—The Kid's "Castle"—Interview with Bowdre—A Mexican Bully—San Miguel Officers—Reinforcements from the Canadian

The Country between Fort Sumner and Las Cañaditas, was well known to me, and, in order to approach the ranch unobserved, we took across the prairie, designing to make observations from the surrounding hills through our field glasses. When yet some eight miles distant from the ranch, we discovered a horse-man riding in that direction, evidently coming from another ranch about twelve miles from Fort Sumner, and bound for Las Cañaditas. He was a long distance from us, but with the assistance of excellent field glasses we recognized Tom O. Foliard. There was a pass through the hills, unknown to all our party except myself, which would surely intercept him if we could get through in time. This was a "hard road to travel." It was overgrown with weeds and brush and encumbered with loose rock, rendering it almost impassable. With much difficulty we made through the path and came out on the beaten road within three hundred yards of Foliard, who had not before suspected our presence. He was equal to the situation. Soon as he saw us the splendid animal he rode sprang away under whip and spur, and his Winchester pumped lead fast and furious as he ran. We pursued, but, instead of riding on to him, as I had anticipated, he left us like the wind. He fired twenty-six shots, as he afterwards declared. I fired but three times. There were but Lawton and Mitchell with me, as the others had fallen behind in the almost inaccessible ravine. These two used their rifles industriously. No harm was done by this fusillade on either side, except that Foliard's horse was wounded in the thigh. He made a splendid run and a brave horseback fight, reaching the ranch and giving the alarm in time, as when we reached there the birds had flown to the hills.

We were not sure whether Foliard had succeeded in reaching the ranch, and if he had, presumed the party might remain and give us a fight. So we approached with caution. Lawton, Mason, McKinney, and Roberts, only, were with me, as I had sent Mitchell back to bring up the rear. I proposed to divide what force we had and charge on the house. I was overruled. My companions advised to await the rest of the posse. When we did walk up to the ranch, unopposed, our precautions appeared rather ludicrous to us, as we only found Bowdre's wife and another Mexican woman, who hailed our advent with "terror-born lamentations." Our labor, however, was not without its reward, as we captured a pair of mules stolen from a stage company on the Rio Grande by Mose Dedrick, and by him turned over to The Kid. We also secured four stolen horses.

We returned to Fort Sumner, stayed one night, and relieving guard over the prisoners, started for The Kid's stronghold, Los Portales, where he was wont to harbor his stolen stock. This is sixty miles east of Fort Sumner and is the veritable castle so graphically described by newspaper correspondents; its approaches impassable except to the initiated—inaccessible and impregnable to foes. Here is where romance has surrounded the young brigand with more than oriental luxury, blest him with the loves of female beauties whose charm would shame the fairest tenant of an eastern seraglio, and clothed him in gorgeous splendor. It seems cruel to rob this fairy castle of its magnificence, to steal the romance from so artfully woven a tale; but the naked facts are:—Los Portales is but a small cave in a quarry of rock, not more than fifteen feet high, lying out and obstructing the view across a beautiful level prairie, and bubbling up, near the rocks, are two springs of cool clear water, furnishing an ample supply for at least one thousand head of cattle. There is no building nor corral. All signs of habitation are a snubbing post, some rough working utensils and a pile of blankets. "Just that and nothing more."

The Kid had about sixty head of cattle in the vicinity of Los Portales, all but eight of which were stolen from John Newcomb at *Agua Azul.* We found only two cows and calves and a yearling, and heard afterwards that The Kid had moved his stock to another spring about fifteen miles east. We had brought no provisions with us and found only some musty flour and a little salt in the cave. We killed the yearling and banqueted on beef straight while there. The next day we circled the camp, found no more stock, and, after an absence of four days, returned to Fort Sumner.

On our return trip we took dinner at Wilcox's ranch, twelve miles from the Fort. Wilcox told me that Bowdre was very anxious to have an interview with me. He wanted to see if he could get bonds in case he came in and gave himself up. I left word with Wilcox for Bowdre to meet me at the forks of the road, two miles from Sumner, at two o'clock the following day. He kept the appointment, and I showed him a letter from Capt. J. C. Lea, of Roswell, wherein it was promised that if he, Bowdre, would change his evil life and forsake his disreputable associates, every effort would be made by good citizens to procure his release on bail and give him an opportunity to redeem himself.

Bowdre did not seem to place much faith in these promises, and evidently thought I was playing a game to get him in my power. He, however, promised to cease all commerce with The Kid and his gang. He said he could not help but feed them when they came to his ranch, but that he would not harbor them more than he could help. I told him if he did not quit them or surrender, he would be pretty sure to get captured or killed, as we were after the gang and would sleep on their trail until we took them in, dead or alive. And thus we parted.

On my arrival at Fort Sumner I dismissed the posse, except Mason, and they returned to Roswell. I hired C. B. Hoadley to convey the prisoners to Las Vegas. On my arrival at Sumner with them from below, I had written to Desiderio Romero, sheriff of San Miguel County, advising him that I had them under guard at Fort Sumner and requesting him to come after them. I had heard nothing from him, and concluded to take them to Las Vegas myself, and get them off my hands. The day we were to start, Juan Roibal and two other Mexicans came into Sumner from Puerto de Luna to inquire about the horses of Grzelachowski stolen by The Kid. They returned as far as Gayheart's ranch with us, assisting Mason and myself to guard the prisoners. At Gayheart's they took the direct route to Puerto de Luna, and, after some delay, we started by the right-hand road. We were only three or four miles on our way when a messenger from Roibal intercepted us with information that a sheriff's posse, from Las Vegas, were at Puerto de Luna on their way to Fort Sumner after the prisoners.

This changed my route and I took the other road. We met the Las Vegas posse about eight miles from Puerto de Luna. They were led by two deputy sheriffs, Francisco Romero and a Dutchman—and he was a Dutchman. They had arrived at Puerto de Luna with three men, in a spring wagon, and had there swelled the party of five to twenty or twenty-five, all Mexicans, except the irrepressible Dutchman. Discarding the wagon, they were all mounted, and came down upon my little party like a whirlwind of lunatics—their steeds prancing and curveting—with loud boasts and swaggering airs—one would have thought they had taken a contract to fight the battle of Valverde over again, and that an army of ten thousand rebels opposed them instead of two manacled prisoners.

At Puerto de Luna the deputies receipted to me for the prisoners, and, as I was turning them over, Webb accosted me and said he had but $10 in the world, but would give me that if I would accompany him to Las Vegas; that he thought it was my duty to do so, as I had arrested him, and he never would have surrendered to such a mob as this. I replied that if he looked at it in that light, and feared for his safety—I would go on, but, of course, refused his money.

The deputies took the prisoners to have them ironed. I was sitting in the store of A. Grzelachowski, when Juanito Maes, a noted desperado, thief, and murderer, approached me, threw up his hands and said he had heard I wanted him and had come to surrender. I replied that I did not know him, had no warrant for him, and did not want him. As Maes left me a Mexican named Mariano Leiva, the big bully of the town, entered, his hand on a pistol in his pocket, walked up to me, and said he would like to see any d–d Gringo arrest him. I told him to go away and not annoy me. He went out on the porch, where he continued in a tirade of abuse, all directed against me.

I finally went out and told him that I had no papers for him and no business with him, that whenever I did have he would not be put to the trouble of hunting me, that I would be sure to find him. With an oath, he raised his left arm in a threatening manner, his right hand still on his pistol. I slapped him off the porch. He landed on his feet, drew his pistol and fired without effect. My pistol went off prematurely, the ball striking at his feet–the second shot went through his shoulder, when he turned and ran, firing back as he went, way wide of the mark.

I entered the store and got my Winchester. In a few moments Deputy Romero came in and informed me that I was his prisoner. I brushed him aside and told him I did not propose to submit, asking him the cause of my arrest. He said it was for shooting at Leiva, and reached for my gun. I told him I had no intention of evading the law, but he could not disarm me; that I did not know what sort of mob I had struck; that one man had already deliberately shot at me, and I proposed to keep my arms and protect myself. Mason had come in, and now picked up his rifle and said: "Shall I cut the son-of-a- —— in two, Pat?" I told him not to shoot, that I did not mind the barking of these curs. My friend, Grzelachowski, interfered in my defense and the bold deputy retired. I went to an *Alcalde* the next morning, had an examination, and was discharged.

Deputy Romero had written to the sheriff at Las Vegas that he had arrested the two prisoners, and was on his way up with them, and, also, had Barney Mason, one of The Kid's gang, in charge. The sheriff immediately started his brother, with five or six men, to meet us at Major Hay's ranch. They came in all the paraphernalia of war; if possible, a more ludicrously bombastic mob than the one inaugurated at Puerto de Luna. Threats and oaths and shouts made a pandemonium there. The Romero who had just joined us swore that he had once arrested The Kid at Anton Chico (which was a lie, notwithstanding he proved it by his posse), that he wanted no weapons to arrest The Kid–all he wanted was to get his eyes on him. And yet it is pretty sure that this poodle would have ridden all night to avoid sleeping within ten miles of an old camp of The Kid's.

Rudabaugh once remarked that it only required lightning-bugs and corn-cobs to stampede officers of Las Vegas or Puerto de Luna.

Before we reached Hay's ranch, I had heard that Frank Stewart, agent for cattle-owners on the Canadian, with a numerous party, was at or near Anton Chico, and was on the trail of The Kid and his band; that he wanted to recover some stock stolen by them, but would much rather have the thieves. On this information I had started Mason to Anton Chico with a message for Stewart. The Las Vegas deputies offered objections to his leaving the posse, as they had, by some process of reasoning, got it in their heads that Mason was their prisoner, although they had no warrant for him and had not arrested him. I paid no attention to their senseless gabble, except to tell them that Mason would be in Las Vegas nearly as soon as we would, and if they wanted him then, they could arrest him. I pointed him out to the sheriff, a few days afterwards, in Las Vegas, but they had changed their minds and did not want him.

A few miles from Las Vegas, this delectable posse stopped at a wayside *tendejon* to hoist in a cargo of *aguardiente;* I seized the opportunity to escape their objectionable society, and rode on, alone, into the town. I was ashamed to be seen with the noisy, gabbling, boasting, senseless, undignified mob, whose deportment would have disgusted The Kid and his band of thieves.

CHAPTER XVIII.

Frank Stewart—Organizing for the Hunt—A Modern Don Quixote—A Trustworthy Spy—On the Trail

As Mason and myself had left the direct road from Fort Sumner to Las Vegas to meet the officers at Puerta de Luna, we missed The Kid, Rudabaugh, and Wilson, who were then on their way to Las Cañaditas, as heretofore related. I had understood that Frank Stewart, the agent of Panhandle stockmen, was going below to hunt The Kid, and my message, sent to him at Anton Chico by Mason, mentioned in the last chapter, was to the effect that I wanted to see him before he started. He came, with Mason, and met me at Las Vegas, but had sent his party on to White Oaks.

Stewart had planned to search in the vicinity of White Oaks, and, should he miss the gang there, to cut across the mountains, strike the Rio Pecos below, and follow it up. I opposed this course, as giving the outlaws time to leave the country or seek a safe hiding place. Stewart was convinced that his plan would not work, and, about one o'clock, p.m., on the 14th day of December, 1880, Stewart, Mason, and myself left Las Vegas to overtake Stewart's posse and turn them back. We stopped at Hay's ranch, eighteen miles from Las Vegas, got supper, and continued our ride. About one o'clock at night we fell in with some Mexican freighters, camped by the roadside, and slept until daylight. We rode hard until about nine o'clock on the morning of the 15th, when we hove in sight of Stewart's party.

Whilst eating a hearty breakfast, Stewart, who wanted to sound the disposition of his men but did not wish to confide all our plans to them, said:

"Boys, there is a bunch of steers down near Fort Sumner, which I am anxious to round up and take in."

They all dropped on the class of property he was after, and a few of them weakened when they understood that a conflict with The Kid and his desperate band was, probably, impending, whilst others were more than willing to take a hand.

At last Stewart said: "Do as you please, boys, but there is no time to talk. Those who are going with me, get ready at once. I want no man who hesitates."

In a moment, Lon. Chambers, Lee Halls, Jim East, "Poker Tom," "The Animal," and "Tenderfoot Bob" were in the saddle ready to accompany us.

We took a southwesterly direction, aiming to strike the Rio Pecos at Puerto de Luna. We made about forty-five miles that day and pulled up at a Mexican ranch about nine o'clock at night, some fifteen miles north of Puerto de Luna, where we found entertainment for neither man nor beast. We, however, consoled ourselves with remembrances of buffalo humps we had consumed in days past, and feasted on anticipation of good cheer on the morrow.

On the morning of the 16th, we took the road at daylight. It was intensely cold, and some of our party walked, leading their horses, to save their feet. Between eight and nine o'clock we drew up in front of Grzelachowski's store, were cordially welcomed and hospitably entertained. To rest and save our horses we determined to lay over until the next morning. We spent the day infusing warmth into our chilled bodies and through the medium of mesquite-root fires and internal applications of liquid fuel, and in eating apples and drawing corks. We were entertained by the vaporings of one Francisco Arragon, who was a veritable Don Quixote—with his mouth. Over and over again, he took in The Kid and all his band—each time in questionable Spanish. His weapons were eloquence, fluency, and well-emphasized oaths, inspired by frequent potations of a mixed character. This great brave did not take to me kindly, but lavished all his surplus affection, attention, and maudlin sentiment on Stewart and Mason, and threw before them the aegis of his prowess and infallibility. At last he invited my two companions to accompany him to his house, "just across the street," where he promised to regale them with rock and rye, *ad infinitum*. Little persuasion was necessary to start my friends. The rock and rye was produced, and after two or three libations, Don Francisco opened his combat with the windmills. It was his philosophy that, as they were run by wind, they must be fought by wind and he launched whole tornadoes against invisible foes. It was evidently the object of this hero to impress the wife of his bosom with his bravery, and he succeeded to such an extent that his ravings elicited from her a thousand impassioned entreaties that he would stay his dreadful hand and refrain from annihilating The Kid and all his cohorts, thus endangering his own precious life. This was what Arragon was playing for, and, if she had failed to exhibit distress and alarm he would, doubtless, have hammered her black and blue so soon as he had her alone. And yet her entreaties only redoubled his profane threatenings. He was eager to get at the bloody desperadoes. He wanted me, nor none of my party to accompany him. He, alone, would do all the fighting; would round them up, bring them in, and turn them over to me. He seemed to think Americans were scarce, and he wanted to save them. He was going to get me all the volunteers I wanted in the morning–ten, twenty, or thirty. After fighting this range battle until near night, he concluded to start out immediately, and bring them in right away; that they would take shelter when they saw him coming, but he would tear the walls down over their heads and drag them out by the heels. At last, the trio, Stewart, Mason, and the wife, elicited from him a solemn pledge that he would give The Kid and his followers a few hour's lease of life.

In the morning I thought I would waste a little time and see if I could get this doughty ally along. Stewart begged that he might be allowed to go, just to see how he did it. He said he would be ready at ten o'clock, and mounting his horse he rode furiously up and down the streets and plaza pretending to be enlisting recruits, but secretly dissuading citizens from going. At ten o'clock we asked him if he was ready. He was not, but would be almost immediately. About two o'clock, the bold Arragon announced that he had no legal right to interfere with the outlaws and declined to accompany us. It was with difficulty I prevented Stewart from roping and dragging him by the horn of his saddle.

We got away from Puerto de Luna about three o'clock in the evening, with but one recruit–Juan Roibal. Of all the cowardly braggarts, not one could be induced to go when the time came. They were willing to ride in any direction but that in which The Kid might be encountered. I must, however, except two young men, Americans, Charlie Rudolph and George Wilson, who did not start with us, having neither horses nor arms; but, ashamed of the pusillanimity of their townsmen, they borrowed horses and arms and overtook us at John Gayheart's ranch, eighteen miles below Puerto de Luna and twenty-five above Fort Sumner. We reached here about nine o'clock in the night of December 17th in a terrible snow storm from the northwest.

At Gayheart's we got a lunch, rested a while, and by twelve o'clock were again in the saddle, with a ride of twenty-five miles before us, which we were determined to make by daylight. I had started a spy, Jose Roibal, brother to Juan, from Puerto de Luna to Fort Sumner the day previous. He was a trustworthy fellow, recommended to me by Grzelachowski. He had ridden straight through to Fort Sumner without stopping, obtained all the information possible, and, on his return, met me at Pablo Beaubien's ranch, a mile above Gayheart's, where he reported.

His appearance at Fort Sumner excited no suspicion. He kept his eyes open and his mouth closed. When necessary to talk he pretended to be a sheep-herder looking for strays. It was a sure thing that The Kid, with five adherents, was at Fort Sumner and that he was on the *que vive*. George Farnum, a buckboard driver, had told him that Mason and myself were on the way down, but neither of them knew that we were not alone. They kept horses saddled, and were prepared to "take us in," when we should heave in sight, or to run, as occasion demanded.

After gaining all the information possible, without exciting suspicion, Jose rode leisurely out from Fort Sumner, crossing the river on the west. Foliard and Pickett followed him across the river and asked him who he was, his business, etc. He replied that he was a herder and was hunting stray sheep. His interlocutors seemed satisfied, and allowed him to depart.

The Kid, Foliard, Bowdre, Rudabaugh, Wilson, and Pickett, after their meeting at Las Cañaditas, had gone directly to Fort Sumner, and were there putting in a gay time at cards, drinking, and dancing. The Kid had heard of the capture of mules and other stolen stock at Yerby's ranch, and was terribly angered thereat. The gang had squandered many precious hours in cursing me, and threatening me with bloody death. The Kid had written to Capt. Lea, at Roswell, that if the officers would give him a little time, and let him alone until he could rest up his horses and get ready, he would leave the country for good; but if he was pursued, or harassed, he would inaugurate a bloody war and fight it out to the fatal end.

With this information from our faithful spy, we left Gayheart's ranch about midnight, reaching Fort Sumner just before daylight. I camped the outfit a little above the plaza, took Mason with me, and went prospecting. We understood that the outlaws kept their horses at A. H. Smith's corral when in Sumner, and we first visited him. We found that their horses were not there, then wakened Smith, who told us that they had left after dark the night before. We all turned in at Smith's except Mason, who went to the house of his father-in-law. He returned, however, immediately, and said he had heard that The Kid and gang were in an old deserted building near by. This report served to excite us, rouse us out of bed, and disappoint us, as there was no one at the house designated. We concluded we would, per force, possess our souls in patience until daylight.

CHAPTER XIX.

The Kid's Accomplices—The Trap—Foliard Mortally Wounded—"Kill Me, Pat, and Put Me Out of Misery"—Death—Flight—Pursuit—A Lunatic from Fright—The Kid Again Escapes Death and Arrest

As soon as any one was stirring in the plaza of Fort Sumner on the morning of the 18th, I left our party, except Mason, in concealment and started out to take observations. I met a Mexican named Iginio Garcia, in my rounds, whom I knew to be a tool of The Kid's, and spoke to him. I warned him not to betray my presence to any of the gang and not to leave the plaza. He represented that he had urgent business below, but assured me that he would keep my counsel. I consented that he should go, as it did not matter much. If they knew I was there, they would labor under the impression that my only support in an engagement would be Mason and, perhaps, a Mexican or two. The fact of the presence of Stewart and his party, I felt sure had not been betrayed. Garcia lived twelve miles south of Fort Sumner, and started in that direction.

A day or two previous to these events, A. H. Smith had sent Bob. Campbell and Jose Valdez to Bosque Grande, to drive up a bunch of milch cows which he had bought from Dan. Dedrick. Garcia met these two near his home. He knew that Campbell was a friend and accomplice of The Kid and that Valdez was, at least, a friend. He told them that I was at Fort Sumner, and they immediately turned the cows loose and separated; Campbell went to a camp close by, hired a Mexican boy, and sent him to The Kid with a note. The Kid and gang were at Wilcox's ranch, twelve miles east of Sumner. Valdez rode into Sumner, where I met him and inquired if he had seen Garcia. He said he saw him at a distance, but did not speak to him. I asked no further questions, as I was convinced I would get no word of truth from him.

On receipt of Campbell's note, The Kid sent Juan, a stepson of Wilcox, to the Fort to see how the land lay, with instructions to return and report as soon as possible. Wilcox and his partner, Brazil, were law-abiding citizens and, subsequently, rendered me invaluable assistance in my efforts to capture the gang; but had they been betrayed to The Kid, he would have killed them without compunction. Seeing Juan in the plaza, I suspected his errand, accosted him, and found my surmise was correct. After a little conversation I concluded that I would fully trust him. I made known my business to him; he promised to faithfully follow my instructions, and I believed him. I gleaned from this messenger the following information.

The Kid and all his band had intended to come to Fort Sumner the following day in a wagon, with a load of beef. The Kid had, that morning, received a note from Bob. Campbell, by a Mexican boy, wherein Bob. related how he and Valdez met Garcia, and that Garcia had notified them of my presence at Sumner. Hence Valdez had lied to me. This note disarranged The Kid's plans, and he had sent Juan in to try to learn something of my movements, number of my force, etc. I asked Juan if he would work with me to deceive the outlaws. He said he would do anything I told him. I left him and went to Valdez. I made him write a note to The Kid saying that I and all my party had gone to Roswell, and there was no danger. I then wrote a note to Wilcox and Brazil, stating that I was at Fort Sumner with thirteen men, that I was on the trail of The Kid and gang, and that I would never let up until I got them, or run them out of the country, and asking them to cooperate with me. So soon as Juan had transacted his business in the plaza, he came to me; I gave him the two notes, warning him not to get them mixed, and started him home.

The Kid and party were impatiently awaiting Juan's return. They scanned Valdez's note eagerly—then shouted their scorn at my timidity; said this news was too good for them; that they had intended to come in after me any how; had a good will to follow us; if they could kill me, they would not be further molested; if we had not run away, they would have "shot us up a lot," and set us on foot. Juan was not asleep and, when opportunity served, gave the other note to Wilcox.

I was confident that the gang would be in Fort Sumner that night, and made arrangements to receive them. There was an old hospital building on the eastern boundary of the plaza—the direction from which they would come—the wife of Bowdre occupied a room of the building, and I felt sure they would pay their first visit to her. I took my posse there, placed a guard about the house, and awaited the game.

They came fully two hours before we expected them. We were passing away the time playing cards. There were several Mexicans in the plaza, some of whom, I feared, would convey information to the gang, as I had them with me, in custody. Snow was lying on the ground, increasing the light outside. About eight o'clock a guard cautiously called from the door:—"Pat, some one is coming!" "Get your guns, boys," said I; "None but the men we want are riding this time of night."

The Kid, with all his reckless bravery, had a strong infusion of caution in his composition when not excited. He afterwards told me that as they approached the building that night he was riding in front with Foliard. As they bore down close upon us, he said, a strong suspicion arose in his mind that they might be running into unseen danger. "Well," said I, "what did you do?" He replied:—"I wanted a chew of tobacco, bad. Wilson had some that was good, and he was in the rear. I went back after tobacco, don't you see?" and his eye twinkled mischievously.

One of the Mexicans followed me out, and we two joined the guard, Lon. Chambers, on one side, and Mason, with the rest of the party, went round the building to intercept them should they aim to pass on into the plaza. The gang were in full sight approaching. In front rode Foliard and Pickett. I was under the porch and close against the wall, partly hidden by some harness hanging there, Chambers close behind me, and the Mexican behind him. I whispered:—"That's them." They rode up until Foliard's horse's head was under the porch, when I called, "Halt?" Foliard reached for his pistol—Chambers and I both fired; his horse wheeled and ran at least one hundred and fifty yards. Quick as possible I fired at Pickett. The flash of Chambers' gun disconcerted my aim, and I missed him; but one would have thought, by the way he ran and yelled, that he had a dozen balls in him. When Foliard's horse ran with him, he was uttering cries of mortal agony, and we were convinced that he had received his death. He, however, wheeled his horse and, as he rode slowly back, he said:—"Don't shoot, Garrett. I'm killed." Mason called—"Take your medicine old boy, take your medicine," and was going to Foliard. I called to Mason and told him that he was killed, and might want revenge. He could pull a trigger yet, and to be careful how he approached him. I called to Tom to throw up his hands, that I would give him no chance to kill me. He said he was dying and could not throw up his hands, and begged that we would take him off his horse and let him die as easy as possible. Holding our guns down on him we went up, took his gun out of the scabbard, lifted him off his horse, carried him into the house and laid him down, took off his pistol, which was full-cocked, and found that he was shot through the left side, just below the heart, and his coat was cut across the front by a bullet. During this encounter with Foliard and Pickett, the party on the other side had seen The Kid and the rest of the gang, had fired on them and killed Rudabaugh's horse, which, however, ran twelve miles with him, to Wilcox's ranch, before he died. Soon as Mason and his party fired, these four ran like a bunch of wild Nueces steers. They were completely surprised and demoralized. As soon as The Kid and companions disappeared, Mason came round the building just as Foliard was returning, reeling in his saddle. After we had laid him down inside, he begged me to kill him, said if I was a friend of his I would put him out of his misery. I told him I was no friend to men of his kind who sought to murder me because I tried to do my duty, and that I did not shoot up my friends as he was shot. Just then Mason entered the room again. He changed his tone at once and cried:—"Don't shoot any more, for God's sake, I'm already killed." Perhaps he guessed that if he called on Mason to put him out of his misery, he would comply with his request. Mason told him again to "take his medicine." He replied:—"It's the best medicine I ever took." He also asked Mason to tell McKinney to write to his grandmother in Texas, and inform her of his death. Once he exclaimed:—"O! my God, is it possible I must die?" I said to him, just before he died:—"Tom, your time is short." He answered:—"The sooner the better: I will be out of pain." He censured no one, but told who were there with him. He died in about three quarters of an hour after he was shot.

Pickett was unhurt, but was nearly scared to death. He went howling over the prairie, yelling bloody murder, and was lost until the next night. He ran his horse down and then took it on foot, reached Wilcox's ranch about dark the next night, and hid in a haystack. He had run his horse full twenty-five miles in a northeast direction, before he gave out, and then walked twelve or fifteen miles to the ranch. Here he remained, crouching in fear and trembling in the hay-stack, until he saw his companions ride in from the hill.

The Kid, Rudabaugh, Bowdre, and Wilson fled to Wilcox's ranch, where Rudabaugh got another horse. They then lost no time in getting to the hills, from which they watched the ranch and surrounding country throughout all the next day with their field glasses. At dark they rode back to the house, when Pickett showed himself. It must have been amusing to witness this fellow's sudden change from abject cowardice to excessive bravado so soon as he realized that he was actually alive and unharmed, and that he had friends within reach to whom he could look for protection. He swaggered about and blowed his bugle something in this strain. "Boys, I got that d—d long-legged fellow that hollered, 'Halt.' I had my gun lying on my saddle, in front of me, and, just as he hailed, I poured it into him. O, I got him sure."

The gang, now reduced to five, remained at Wilcox's that night. They were depressed and disheartened. After a long consultation, they concluded to send some one to Fort Sumner the following morning to spy out the lay of the land. They relieved guard through the night to prevent surprise and sent Wilcox's partner, Mr. Brazil, to the plaza the next day. They had suspected Wilcox and Brazil of treachery, when they were so effectually surprised at the hospital building, but had been entirely reassured by them since their return.

CHAPTER XX.

The Kid and Gang Trapped Again—Death of Bowdre—The Outlaws—Desperate Plans to Escape—Their Way Blockaded by the Body of a Dead Horse-Surrender—Remnant of The Gang Landed in Jail at Las Vegas

Brazil came to me at Fort Sumner on the morning of December 20th. He described the condition of the crestfallen band and told me they had sent him in to take items and report to them. I told him to return and tell them that I was at Sumner with only Mason and three Mexicans, that I was considerably scared up and wanted to go back to Roswell, but feared to leave the plaza. Brazil did not return until the following day. When he was ready to start, I told him if he found the gang at the ranch when he arrived there, to remain. If they had left, or did leave, after his arrival, to come and report to me; that, if he did not come to me sooner, I would start for the ranch at two o'clock in the morning; and, that, if I did not meet him on the road, I would feel sure they were at the ranch.

This faithful friend went home and returned, reaching Sumner about twelve o'clock in the night. There was snow on the ground, it was desperately cold, and Brazil's beard was full of icicles. He reported that The Kid and his four companions had taken supper at Wilcox's, then mounted, and left. We all started for the ranch. I sent Brazil ahead to see whether the gang had returned, whilst, with my posse, I took a circuitous route by Lake Ranch, a mile or two off the road, thinking they might be there. We rounded up the house, found it vacant, and rode on towards Wilcox's. About three miles from there we met Brazil. He said the outlaws had not returned and showed me their trail on the snow. After following this trail a short distance, I was convinced that they had made for Stinking Springs, where was an old deserted house built by Alejandro Perea. When within a half-mile of the house, we halted and held a consultation. I told my companions I was confident we had them trapped, and cautioned them to preserve silence. When within about four hundred yards, we divided our party and left Juan Roibal in charge of the horses. With one-half the force I circled the house. Finding a dry arroyo, we took its bed and were able to approach pretty close. Stewart, with the rest of the posse, found concealment within about two hundred yards of the building on the other side. There were three horses tied to projecting rafters of the house, and, knowing that there were five of the gang, and that they were all mounted when they left Wilcox's, we concluded they had led two horses inside. There was no door; only an opening, where a door had once been. I sent a messenger, who crept around to Stewart, proposing that, as they were surely there, we should stealthily enter the house, cover them with our guns, and hold them until daylight. Stewart demurred. Lee Hall was in favor of the plan. Shivering with cold, we awaited daylight or a movement from the inmates of the house.

I had a perfect description of The Kid's dress, especially his hat. I had told all the posse that, should The Kid make his appearance, it was my intention to kill him, and the rest would surrender. The Kid had sworn that he would never yield himself a prisoner, but would die fighting, with a revolver at each ear, and I knew he would keep his word. I was in a position to command a view of the doorway, and told my men that when I brought up my gun, to all raise and fire.

Before it was fairly daylight, a man appeared at the entrance with a nose bag in his hand, whom I firmly believed to be The Kid. His size and dress, especially the hat, corresponded with his description exactly. I gave the signal by bringing my gun to my shoulder, my men raised, and seven bullets sped on their errand of death. Our victim was Charley Bowdre. Turning, he reeled back into the house. In a moment Wilson's voice was heard. He called to me and said that Bowdre was killed and wanted to come out. I told him to come out with his hands up. As he started, The Kid caught hold of his belt, drew his revolver around in front of him and said:—"They have murdered you, Charley, but you can get revenge. Kill some of the sons-of —— before you die." Bowdre came out, his pistol still hanging in front of him, but with his hands up. He walked towards our ranks until he recognized me, then came straight to me, motioned with his hand towards the house, and strangling with blood, said:—"I wish—I wish—I wish—" then, in a whisper:—"I'm dying!" I took hold of him, laid him gently on my blankets, and he died almost immediately.

Watching every movement about the house in the increasing light, I shortly saw a motion of one of the ropes by which the horses were tied, and dropped on the fact that they were attempting to lead one of them inside. My first impulse was to shoot the rope in two, but it was shaking so, I feared to miss. I did better—just as the horse was fairly in the opening, I shot him and he fell dead, partially barricading the outlet. To prevent another attempt of this kind, I shot the ropes in two which held the other two horses, and they walked away. They still had two horses in the house, one of them The Kid's favorite mare, celebrated for speed, bottom, and beauty.

I now opened a conversation with the besieged, of whom The Kid was spokesman. I asked him how he was fixed in there.

"Pretty well," answered The Kid, "but we have no wood to get breakfast."

"Come out," said I, "and get some. Be a little sociable."

"Can't do it, Pat," replied he. "Business is too confining. No time to run around."

"Didn't you fellows forget a part of your programme yesterday?" said I. "You know you were to come in on us at Fort Sumner, from some other direction, give us a square fight, set us afoot, and drive us down the Pecos."

Brazil told me that when he took the information to The Kid that I only had Mason and three Mexicans with me at Sumner, and was afraid to leave for home, he proposed to come and take me in. Bowdre had objected to the expedition. My banter caused The Kid to drop on the fact that they had been betrayed, and he became reticent.

Our party were becoming very hungry, and, getting together, we arranged to go to Wilcox's ranch for breakfast. I went first, with one-half the men. The distance was only about three miles. When we reached there, Brazil asked me what news I brought. I told him the news was bad, that we had killed the very man we did not want to kill. When he learned that it was Bowdre, he said:—"I don't see why you should be sorry for having killed him. After you had the interview with him the other day, and was doing your best to get him out of his troubles, he said to me, as we were riding home, 'I wish you would get that d—d long-legged son-of-a —— out to meet me once more; I would just kill him and end all this trouble!' Now, how sorry are you?"

I made arrangements with Wilcox to haul out to our camp some provisions, wood, and forage for our horses. I did not know how long the outlaws might hold out, and concluded I would make it as comfortable as possible for myself and the boys. Charley Rudolph had frozen his feet slightly the night previous. On my return, Stewart and the balance of the boys went to breakfast.

About three o'clock the gang turned loose the two horses from the inside. We picked them up, as we had the other two. About four o'clock the wagon arrived from Wilcox's with provisions and wood. We built a rousing fire and went to cooking. The odor of roasting meat was too much for the famished lads, who were without provisions. Craving stomachs overcame brave hearts. Rudabaugh stuck out from the window a handkerchief that had once been white, at the end of a stick, and called to us that they wanted to surrender. I told them that they could all come out with their hands up, if they wanted to. Rudabaugh then came out to our camp and said they would all surrender if I would guarantee them protection from violence. This, of course, I did. Rudabaugh returned to the house, where they held a short consultation. In a few moments they all, The Kid, Wilson, Pickett, and Rudabaugh, came out, were disarmed, got their supper, and we took them to Wilcox's. I sent Brazil, Mason, and Rudolph back to the ranch with a wagon after the body of Bowdre. On their arrival with the corpse at Wilcox's ranch, the cortege started for Fort Sumner, getting there before night. We turned Bowdre's body over to his wife, ironed the prisoners, and by sundown Stewart, Mason, Jim East, "Poker Tom," and myself, with the prisoners in charge, started for Las Vegas.

The Kid and Rudabaugh were cheerful and gay during the trip. Wilson seemed dejected, and Pickett frightened. The Kid said that, had they succeeded in leading the three horses, or two of them, or one of them, into the house, they would have made a break to get away. He said, also, that he, alone, would have made a target of himself until his mare could have carried him out of range of our guns, or we had killed him, if it had not been for the dead horse barring his way. He said he knew she would not try to pass that, and, if she did, she would have knocked the top of his head off against the lintel of the doorway. Whilst at Fort Sumner, The Kid had made Stewart a present of the mare, remarking that he expected his business would be so confining for the next few months that he would hardly find time for horse-back exercise.

We reached Gayheart's ranch, with our prisoners, about midnight, rested until eight in the morning, and reached Puerto de Luna about two o'clock p.m., on Christmas day. My friend Grzelachowski gave us all a splendid dinner. My ubiquitous Don Quixote Aragon proffered to me, again, his invaluable services and that of his original mob, which I respectfully declined.

With a fresh team, we got away from Puerto de Luna about four o'clock, broke our wagon, borrowed one of Capt. Clarency, and reached Hay's ranch for breakfast. At two o'clock p.m., December 26, we reached Las Vegas and, through a crowd of citizens, made our way to the jail. Our objective point was the Santa Fe jail, as there were United States warrants against all our prisoners except Pickett. Him we intended to leave at Las Vegas. The other three we proposed to go on to Santa Fe with in the morning, although we expected, and so did Rudabaugh, that the authorities at Las Vegas would insist on holding him for the killing of the jailor. We had promised Rudabaugh to take him to Santa Fe, and were determined to do it. So Stewart went and made oath that we were holding this prisoner on a United States warrant; armed with which instrument and our warrant, we intended to hold this prisoner and take him to Santa Fe.

CHAPTER XXI.

A Mob at Las Vegas Want Rudabaugh—The Kid in Jail at Santa Fe—Attempt to Escape—The Kid on Trial at Mesilla for Murder—Sentenced to Hang—Confined at Lincoln

On the Morning of December 27th, I had fresh irons placed on The Kid, Rudabaugh, and Wilson. Michael Cosgrove, Esq., mail contractor, being well acquainted in Santa Fe, I induced him to accompany me there with the prisoners. I therefore released two of my guards, and started with Cosgrove, Stewart, and Mason.

After breakfast we went to the jail for our prisoners. They turned out The Kid and Wilson to us, who were handcuffed together. We demanded Rudabaugh. They refused to yield him up, saying he had escaped from that jail, and they wanted him for murder. I told them that our right to the prisoner ranked theirs, as I was a deputy United States marshal and had arrested Rudabaugh for an offense against laws of the United States, that I knew nothing of any other offense or arrest, that he was my prisoner, I was responsible for him, and intended to have him. Stewart drew his affidavit on them, and they, at last, turned Rudabaugh out to us.

We had been on the train with our three prisoners but a few minutes when we noticed that a good many Mexicans, scattered through the crowd, were armed with rifles and revolvers and seemed considerably excited. Stewart and I concluded their object was to take Rudabaugh off the train. I asked Stewart if we should make a fight for it; he said we would, of course. I said, "Let's make a good one." We felt sure they intended to mob him, or we might have given him up. Besides, he acknowledged that he was afraid of them, and we were pledged to protect him and take him to Santa Fe.

Stewart guarded one door of the car, and I the other. These armed ruffians crowded about the car, but none of them made a formal demand for Rudabaugh, or stated their business. Deputy Sheriff Romero, brother to the sheriff who had so distinguished himself when I brought Webb to him at Hay's ranch, headed a mob of five, who approached the platform where I was standing, flourishing their revolvers. One of the mob said:—"Let's go right in and take him out of there," and they pushed this deputy up on the platform, crowding after him. I merely requested them, in my mildest tones, to get down, and they slid to the ground like a covey of hardback turtles off the banks of the Pecos. They did not seem at all frightened, but modest and bashful-like.

Rudabaugh was excited. The Kid and Wilson seemed unconcerned. I told them not to be uneasy, that we were going to make a fight if they tried to enter the car, and if the fight came off, I would arm them all, and let them take a hand. The Kid's eyes glistened, as he said:—"All right, Pat. All I want is a six-shooter. There is no danger, though. Those fellows won't fight." The mob were weakening and all they wanted was for some one to coax them to desist, so it would not look so much like a square back-down. Some influential Mexicans reasoned a little with them and they subsided. We were detained by them about three-quarters of an hour. I understood, afterwards, that they had presented their guns to the engineer and threatened him if he moved the train. One of the railroad officials threatened them with the law for detaining the United States mail. At last Deputy United States Marshal Mollay mounted the cab and pulled the train out.

I had telegraphed to Deputy United States Marshal Charles Conklin, and found him at the Santa Fe depot, waiting for us. I turned the prisoners over to him, on the 2yth day of December, 1880, and he placed them in the Santa Fe jail. Whilst there they made an attempt to escape by digging a hole through the adobe walls, hiding the dirt under their bedding. This attempt was frustrated through the vigilance of officials.

Rudabaugh was tried and convicted for robbing the United States mail, but no sentence was passed. On demand of territorial authorities he was taken to San Miguel County, tried for the murder of the jailer, convicted, and sentenced to be hung. He took an appeal and now languishes in the Las Vegas jail awaiting a new trial. [He has since escaped.]

Billy Wilson has been twice arraigned for passing counterfeit money, first at Mesilla and then at Santa Fe; but has not, as yet, had a trial. Should he clear himself on this charge, he is in jeopardy for complicity in the murder of Carlyle.

Deputy United States Marshal Tony Neis took The Kid and Wilson from Santa Fe to Mesilla, where The Kid was first tried, at the March, 1881, term of the District Court, for the murder of Roberts at the Mescalero Apache Indian agency, in March, 1878. Judge Bristol assigned Judge Ira E. Leonard, of Lincoln, to defend him. He was acquitted. He was again tried, at the same term, for the murder of Sheriff William Brady, at Lincoln, on the 1st day of April, 1878, and sentenced to be hung on the 13th day of May, 1881, at Lincoln, the county seat of Lincoln County. He was brought from Mesilla by Deputy Marshal Robert Olinger and Deputy Sheriff David Woods, of Doña Ana County, and turned over to me by them at Fort Stanton, nine miles west of Lincoln, April 21, 1881. Lincoln County has never had a jail, until the last few weeks, that would hold a cripple. The county had just purchased the large two-story building, formerly the mercantile house of Murphy & Dolan, for the use of the county as a public building, but no jail had been constructed; hence I was obliged to place a guard over The Kid. I selected Deputy Sheriff J. W. Bell, and Deputy Marshal Robert Olinger, for this duty, and assigned them a guard room in the second story of the county building, separate and apart from other prisoners. This room was at the north-east corner of the building, and one had to pass from a hall, through another large room, to gain the only door to it. There were two windows—one on the north, opening to the street, and the other on the east, opening into a large yard, which ran east a hundred yards, or more, and projected into the street twelve or fourteen feet past the north, or front, walls of the building. At the projecting corner of the yard, next the house on the north-west, was a gate; a path running from this gate along the east end of the building to the rear, or south wall, where was a smaller gate opening into a corral, in the rear of the house. Passing through this corral to the south-west corner of the building, we come to a door leading to a small hall and broad staircase, which was the only, then, means of access to the second story of the building. Facing the north, we ascend five or six steps, reach a square landing, turn to the right, facing the east, and ascend twelve or fourteen steps, reaching the hall which extends through the building from north to south. Turning to the right, we find two doors, one on each side of the hall.

The one to the right leads into a room in the south-west corner of the building, where were kept surplus arms. Turning to the left, from the head of the staircase we find two other doors, one on each side of the hall, and still another at the north end, which opens on a porch, facing the street on the north. The door on the left, or west side of the hall, led to a room appropriated to the confinement of prisoners, over whom I kept a guard. The door on the right, or east side of the hall, opened into a large room, occupied by me as an office, passing through which, another door opens into the north-east apartment, which I assigned to the guard, in which to confine The Kid. The *necessity* of this description will soon be understood by the reader, whether the description is lucid or not.

During the few days The Kid remained in confinement, I had several conversations with him. He appeared to have a plausible excuse for each and every crime charged against him, except, perhaps, the killing of Carlyle. I said to him one day: "Billy, I pass no judgment as to whether your sentence is just for the killing of Brady, but, had you been acquitted on that charge, you would, most surely, have been hung for the murder of Jimmy Carlyle, and I would have pronounced that sentence just. That was the most detestable crime ever charged against you." He seemed abashed and dejected, and only remarked: "There's more about that than people know of." In our conversations, he would sometimes seem on the point of opening his heart, either in confession or justification, but it always ended in an unspoken intimation that it would all be of no avail, as no one would give him credence, and he scorned to beg for sympathy. He expressed no enmity towards me for having been the instrument through which he was brought to justice, but evinced respect and confidence in me, acknowledging that I had only done my duty, without malice, and had treated him with marked leniency and kindness.

As to his guards, he placed confidence in Deputy Sheriff Bell, and appeared to have taken a liking to him. Bell was in no manner connected with the Lincoln County War, and had no animosity or grudge against The Kid. The natural abhorrence of an honest man towards a well-known violator of the law was intensified in Bell's case, by the murder of Carlyle, who was a friend of his; but never, by word or action, did he betray his prejudice, if it existed. As to Deputy Marshal Olinger, the case was altogether different. They had met, opposed in arms, frequently during the past years of anarchy. Bob. Beckwith was a bosom friend of Olinger's—The Kid had killed him. The Kid charged that Olinger had killed friends of his. There existed a reciprocal hatred between these two, and neither attempted to disguise or conceal his antipathy for the other.

CHAPTER XXII.

The Kid's Most Desperate Venture—Liberty over Mangled Corpses—Two Bloody Murders in Thirty Seconds—Thirty-six Buckshot in One Officer's Body—Stands off the Whole Town—Inhabitants Paralyzed with Terror—The Kid Leaves Lincoln Jail Unopposed—Again a Fugitive

On the evening of April 28, 1881, Olinger took all the other prisoners across the street to supper, leaving Bell in charge of The Kid in the guard room. We have but The Kid's tale, and the sparse information elicited from Mr. Geiss, a German employed about the building, to determine the facts in regard to events immediately following Olinger's departure. From circumstances, indications, information from Geiss, and The Kid's admissions, the popular conclusion is that:

At The Kid's request, Bell accompanied him down stairs and into the back corral. As they returned, Bell allowed The Kid to get considerably in advance. As The Kid turned on the landing of the stairs, he was hidden from Bell. He was light and active, and, with a few noiseless bounds, reached the head of the stairs, turned to the right, put his shoulder to the door of the room used as an armory (though locked, this door was well known to open by a firm push), entered, seized a six-shooter, returned to the head of the stairs just as Bell faced him on the landing of the stair-case, some twelve steps beneath, and fired. Bell turned, ran out into the corral and towards the little gate. He fell dead before reaching it. The Kid ran to the window at the south end of the hall, saw Bell fall, then slipped his handcuffs over his hands, threw them at the body, and said:—"Here, d—n you, take these, too." He then ran to my office and got a double-barreled shot-gun. This gun was a very fine one, a breech-loader, and belonged to Olinger. He had loaded it that morning, in presence of The Kid, putting eighteen buckshot in each barrel, and remarked:—"The man that gets one of those loads will feel it." The Kid then entered the guard-room and stationed himself at the east window, opening on the yard.

Olinger heard the shot and started back across the street, accompanied by L. M. Clements. Olinger entered the gate leading into the yard, as Geiss appeared at the little corral gate and said, "Bob, The Kid has killed Bell." At the same instant The Kid's voice was heard above: "Hello, old boy," said he. "Yes, and he's killed me, too," exclaimed Olinger, and fell dead, with eighteen buckshot in his right shoulder and breast and side. The Kid went back through the guard-room, through my office, into the hall, and out on the balcony. From here he could see the body of Olinger, as it lay on the projecting corner of the yard, near the gate. He took deliberate aim and fired the other barrel, the charge taking effect in nearly the same place as the first; then breaking the gun across the railing of the balcony, he threw the pieces at Olinger, saying:—"Take it, d—n you, you won't follow me any more with that gun." He then returned to the back room, armed himself with a Winchester and two revolvers. He was still encumbered with his shackles, but hailing old man Geiss, he commanded him to bring a file. Geiss did so, and threw it up to him in the window. The Kid then ordered the old man to go and saddle a horse that was in the stable, the property of Billy Burt, deputy clerk of probate, then went to a front window, commanding a view of the street, seated himself, and filed the shackles from one leg. Bob. Brookshire came out on the street from the hotel opposite, and started down towards the plaza. The Kid brought his Winchester down on him and said:—"Go back, young fellow, go back. I don't want to hurt you, but I am fighting for my life. I don't want to see anybody leave that house."

In the meantime, Geiss was having trouble with the horse, which broke loose and ran around the corral and yard awhile, but was at last brought to the front of the house. The Kid was all over the building, on the porch, and watching from the windows. He danced about the balcony, laughed, and shouted as though he had not a care on earth. He remained at the house for nearly an hour after the killing before he made a motion to leave. As he approached to mount, the horse again broke loose and ran towards the Rio Bonito. The Kid called to Andrew Nimley, a prisoner, who was standing by, to go and catch him. Nimley hesitated, but a quick, imperative motion by The Kid started him. He brought the horse back and The Kid remarked:—"Old fellow, if you hadn't gone for this horse, I would have killed you." And now he mounted and said to those in hearing:—"Tell Billy Burt I will send his horse back to him," then galloped away, the shackles still hanging to one leg. He was armed with a Winchester and two revolvers. He took the road west, leading to Fort Stanton, but turned north about four miles from town and rode in the direction of Las Tablas.

It is in order to again visit the scene of this tragedy. It was found that Bell was hit under the right arm, the ball passing through the body and coming out under the left arm. On examination it was evident that The Kid had made a very poor shot, for him, and his hitting Bell at all was a scratch. The ball had hit the wall on Bell's right, caromed, passed through his body, and buried itself in an adobe on his left. There was other proof besides the marks on the wall. The ball had surely been indented and creased before it entered the body, as these scars were filled with flesh. The Kid afterwards told Peter Maxwell that Bell shot at him twice and just missed him. There is no doubt but this statement was false. One other shot was heard before Olinger appeared on the scene, but it is believed to have been an accidental one by The Kid whilst prospecting with the arms. Olinger was shot in the right shoulder, breast, and side. He was literally riddled by thirty-six buckshot.

The inhabitants of the whole town of Lincoln appeared to be terror-stricken. The Kid, it is my firm belief, could have ridden up and down the plaza until dark without a shot having been fired at him, nor an attempt made to arrest him. A little sympathy might have actuated some of them, but most of the people were, doubtless, paralyzed with fear when it was whispered that the dreaded desperado, The Kid, was at liberty and had slain his guards.

This, to me, was a most distressing calamity, for which I do not hold myself guiltless. The Kid's escape, and the murder of his two guards, was the result of mismanagement and carelessness, to a great extent. I knew the desperate character of the man whom the authorities would look for at my hands on the 13th day of May—that he was daring and unscrupulous, and that he would sacrifice the lives of a hundred men who stood between him and liberty, when the gallows stared him in the face, with as little compunction as he would kill a coyote. And now realize how all inadequate my precautions were. Yet, in self-defense, and hazarding the charge of shirking the responsibility and laying it upon dead men's shoulders, I must say that my instructions as to caution and the routine of duty were not heeded and followed.

On the bloody 28th of April, I was at White Oaks. I left Lincoln on the day previous to meet engagements to receive taxes. Was at Las Tablas on the 27th, and went from there to White Oaks. On the 29th, I received a letter from John C. Delaney, Esq., of Fort Stanton, merely stating the fact of The Kid's escape and the killing of the guard. The same day Billy Nickey arrived from Lincoln and gave me the particulars. I returned to Lincoln on the 30th, and went out with some volunteer scouts to try and find The Kid's trail, but was unsuccessful. A few days after, Billy Burt's horse came in dragging a rope. The Kid had either turned him loose, or sent him in by some friend, who had brought him into the vicinity of the town and headed him for home.

The next heard of The Kid, after his escapade at Lincoln, was that he had been at Las Tablas and had there stolen a horse from Andy Richardson. He rode this horse to a point a few miles of Fort Sumner, where he got away from him, and The Kid walked into the town. If he made his presence known to any one there, I have not heard of it. At Sumner he stole a horse from Montgomery Bell, who lives some fifty miles above, but was there on business. He rode this horse out of town bareback, going in a southerly direction. Bell supposed the horse had been stolen by some Mexican, and got Barney Mason and Mr. Curington to go with him and hunt him up. Bell left his companions and went down the Rio Pecos. Mason and Curington took another direction. Mason had a rifle and a six-shooter, whilst Curington was unarmed. They came to a Mexican sheep-camp, rode up close to it, and The Kid stepped out and hailed them. The Kid had designated Mason as an object of his direct vengeance. On the sudden and unexpected appearance of The Kid, Mason's business "laid rolling." He had *no sight on his gun,* but wore a *new pair of spurs.* In short, Mason left. Curington stopped and talked to The Kid, who told him that he had Bell's horse, and to tell Bell he was afoot, and must have something to ride out of the country, that, if he could make any other arrangements, he would send the horse to him; if not, he would pay him for it.

It is known that, subsequent to The Kid's interview with Curington, he stayed for some time with one of Pete Maxwell's sheep herders, about thirty-five miles east of Sumner. He spent his time at cow and sheep camps, was often at Cañaditas Arenoso and Fort Sumner. He was almost constantly on the move. And thus, for about two and a half months, The Kid led a fugitive life, hovering, spite of danger, around the scenes of his past two years of lawless adventure. He had many friends who were true to him, harbored him, kept him supplied with territorial newspapers, and with valuable information concerning his safety. The end was not yet, but fast approaching.

CHAPTER XXIII.

Again on the Trail—The Kid Hunted Down—The Fatal Shot in the Dark—The Kid Dies, but Not with His Boots on

During the weeks following The Kid's escape, I was censured by some for my seeming unconcern and inactivity in the matter of his re-arrest. I was egotistical enough to think I knew my own business best, and preferred to accomplish this duty, if possible at all, in my own way. I was constantly, but quietly, at work, seeking sure information and maturing my plans of action. I did not lay about The Kid's old haunts, nor disclose my intentions and operations to any one. I stayed at home, most of the time, and busied myself about the ranch. If my seeming unconcern deceived the people and gave The Kid confidence in his security, my end was accomplished. It was my belief that The Kid was still in the country and haunted the vicinity of Fort Sumner; yet there was some doubt mingled with my belief. He was never taken for a fool, but was credited with the possession of extraordinary forethought and cool judgment, for one of his age. It seemed incredible that, in his situation, with the extreme penalty of law, the reward of detection, and the way of successful flight and safety open to him—with no known tie to bind him to that dangerous locality—it seemed incredible that he should linger in the Territory. My first task was to solve my doubts.

Early in July, I received a reply from a letter I had written to Mr. Brazil. I was at Lincoln when this letter came to me. Mr. Brazil was dodging and hiding from The Kid. He feared his vengeance on account of the part which he, Brazil, had taken in his capture. There were many others who "trembled in their boots" at the knowledge of his escape; but most of them talked him out of his resentment, or conciliated him in some manner.

Brazil's letter gave me no positive information. He said he had not seen The Kid since his escape, but, from many indications, believed he was still in the country. He offered me any assistance in his power to recapture him. I again wrote to Brazil, requesting him to meet me at the mouth of Tayban Arroyo an hour after dark on the night of the 13th day of July.

A gentleman named John W. Poe, who had superseded Frank Stewart, in the employ of the stockmen of the Canadian, was at Lincoln on business, as was one of my deputies, Thomas K. McKinney. I first went to McKinney, and told him I wanted him to accompany me on a business trip to Arizona, that we would go down home and start from there. He consented. I then went to Poe and to him I disclosed my business and all its particulars, showing him my correspondence. He also complied with my request that he should accompany me.

We three went to Roswell and started up the Rio Pecos from there on the night of July l0th. We rode mostly in the night, followed no roads, but taking unfrequented routes, and arrived at the mouth of Tayban Arroyo, five miles south of Fort Sumner one hour after dark on the night of July 13th. Brazil was not there. We waited nearly two hours, but he did not come. We rode off a mile or two, staked our horses, and slept until daylight. Early in the morning we rode up into the hills and prospected awhile with our field glasses.

Poe was a stranger in the county and there was little danger that he would meet any one who knew him at Sumner. So, after an hour or two spent in the hills, he went into Sumner to take observations. I advised him, also, to go on to Sunnyside, seven miles above Sumner, and interview M. Rudolph, Esq., in whose judgment and discretion I had great confidence. I arranged with Poe to meet us that night at moonrise, at La Punta de la Glorietta, four miles north of Fort Sumner. Poe went on to the plaza, and McKinney and myself rode down into the Pecos Valley, where we remained during the day. At night we started out circling around the town and met Poe exactly on time at the trysting place.

Poe's appearance at Sumner had excited no particular observation, and he had gleaned no news there. Rudolph thought, from all indications, that The Kid was about; and yet, at times, he doubted. His cause for doubt seemed to be based on no evidence except the fact that The Kid was no fool, and no man in his senses, under the circumstances, would brave such danger.

I then concluded to go and have a talk with Peter Maxwell, Esq., in whom I felt sure I could rely. We had ridden to within a short distance of Maxwell's grounds when we found a man in camp and stopped. To Poe's great surprise, he recognized in the camper an old friend and former partner, in Texas, named Jacobs. We unsaddled here, got some coffee, and, on foot, entered an orchard which runs from this point down to a row of old buildings, some of them occupied by Mexicans, not more than sixty yards from Maxwell's house. We approached these houses cautiously, and when within ear shot, heard the sound of voices conversing in Spanish. We concealed ourselves quickly and listened; but the distance was too great to hear words, or even distinguish voices. Soon a man arose from the ground, in full view, but too far away to recognize. He wore a broad-brimmed hat, a dark vest and pants, and was in his shirt-sleeves. With a few words, which fell like a murmur on our ears, he went to the fence, jumped it, and walked down towards Maxwell's house.

Little as we then suspected it, this man was The Kid. We learned, subsequently, that, when he left his companions that night, he went to the house of a Mexican friend, pulled off his hat and boots, threw himself on a bed, and commenced reading a newspaper. He soon, however, hailed his friend, who was sleeping in the room, told him to get up and make some coffee, adding:—"Give me a butcher knife and I will go over to Pete's and get some beef; I'm hungry." The Mexican arose, handed him the knife, and The Kid, hatless and in his stocking-feet, started to Maxwell's, which was but a few steps distant.

When The Kid, by me unrecognized, left the orchard, I motioned to my companions, and we cautiously retreated a short distance, and, to avoid the persons whom we had heard at the houses, took another route, approaching Maxwell's house from the opposite direction. When we reached the porch in front of the building, I left Poe and McKinney at the end of the porch, about twenty feet from the door of Pete's room, and went in. It was near midnight and Pete was in bed. I walked to the head of the bed and sat down on it, beside him, near the pillow. I asked him as to the whereabouts of The Kid. He said that The Kid had certainly been about, but he did not know whether he had left or not. At that moment a man sprang quickly into the door, looking back, and called twice in Spanish, "Who comes there?" No one replied and he came on in. He was bareheaded. From his step I could perceive he was either barefooted or in his stocking-feet, and held a revolver in his right hand and a butcher knife in his left.

He came directly towards me. Before he reached the bed, I whispered: "Who is it, Pete?" but received no reply for a moment. It struck me that it might be Pete's brother-in-law, Manuel Abreu, who had seen Poe and McKinney, and wanted to know their business. The intruder came close to me, leaned both hands on the bed, his right hand almost touching my knee, and asked, in a low tone:—"Who are they Pete?"—at the same instant Maxwell whispered to me. "That's him!" Simultaneously The Kid must have seen, or felt, the presence of a third person at the head of the bed. He raised quickly his pistol, a self cocker, within a foot of my breast. Retreating rapidly across the room he cried: "*Quien es? Quien es?*" ("Who's that? Who's that?") All this occurred in a moment. Quickly as possible I drew my revolver and fired, threw my body aside, and fired again. The second shot was useless; The Kid fell dead. He never spoke. A struggle or two, a little strangling sound as he gasped for breath, and The Kid was with his many victims.

Maxwell had plunged over the foot of the bed on the floor, dragging the bed-clothes with him. I went to the door and met Poe and McKinney there. Maxwell rushed past me, out on the porch; they threw their guns down on him, when he cried: "Don't shoot, don't shoot." I told my companions I had got The Kid. They asked me if I had not shot the wrong man. I told them I had made no blunder, that I knew The Kid's voice too well to be mistaken. The Kid was entirely unknown to either of them. They had seen him pass in, and, as he stepped on the porch, McKinney, who was sitting, rose to his feet; one of his spurs caught under the boards, and nearly threw him. The Kid laughed, but probably, saw their guns, as he drew his revolver and sprang into the doorway, as he hailed: "Who comes there?" Seeing a bareheaded, barefooted man, in his shirt-sleeves, with a butcher knife in his hand, and hearing his hail in excellent Spanish, they naturally supposed him to be a Mexican and an *attaché* of the establishment, hence their suspicion that I had shot the wrong man.

We now entered the room and examined the body The ball struck him just above the heart, and must have cut through the ventricles. Poe asked me how many shots I fired; I told him two, but that I had no idea where the second one went. Both Poe and McKinney said The Kid must have fired then, as there were surely three shots fired. I told them that he had fired one shot, between my two. Maxwell said that The Kid fired; yet, when we came to look for bullet marks, none from his pistol could be found. We searched long and faithfully—found both my bullet marks and none other; so, against the impression and senses of four men, we had to conclude that The Kid did not fire at all. We examined his pistol—a self-cocker, calibre 41. It had five cartridges and one shell in the chambers, the hammer resting on the shell, but this proves nothing, as many carry their revolvers in this way for safety; besides, this shell looked as though it had been shot some time before.

It will never be known whether The Kid recognized me or not. If he did, it was the first time, during all his life of peril, that he ever lost his presence of mind, or failed to shoot first and hesitate afterwards. He knew that a meeting with me meant surrender or fight. He told several persons about Sumner that he bore no animosity against me, and had no desire to do me injury. He also said that he knew, should we meet, he would have to surrender, kill me, or get killed himself. So, he declared his intention, should we meet, to commence shooting on sight.

On the following morning, the *Alcalde*, Alejandro Segura, held an inquest on the body. Hon. M. Rudolph, of Sunnyside, was foreman of the coroner's jury. They found a verdict that William H. Bonney came to his death from a gun-shot wound, the weapon in the hands of Pat F. Garrett, that the fatal wound was inflicted by the said Garrett in the discharge of his official duty as sheriff, and that the homicide was justifiable.

The body was neatly and properly dressed and buried in the military cemetery at Fort Sumner, July 15, 1881. His exact age, on the day of his death, was 21 years, 7 months, and 21 days.

I said that the body was buried in the cemetery at Fort Sumner; I wish to add that it is there to-day intact. Skull, fingers, toes, bones, and every hair of the head that was buried with the body on that 15th day of July, doctors, newspaper editors, and paragraphers to the contrary notwithstanding. Some presuming swindlers have claimed to have The Kid's skull on exhibition, or one of his fingers, or some other portion of his body, and one medical gentleman has persuaded credulous idiots that he has all the bones strung upon wires. It is possible that there is a skeleton on exhibition somewhere in the States, or even in this Territory, which was procured somewhere down the Rio Pecos. We have them, lots of them in this section. The banks of the Pecos are dotted from Fort Sumner to the Rio Grande with unmarked graves, and the skeletons are of all sizes, ages, and complexions. Any showman of ghastly curiosities can resurrect one or all of them, and place them on exhibition as the remains of Dick Turpin, Jack Shepherd, Cartouche, or The Kid, with no one to say him nay, so they don't ask the people of the Rio Pecos to believe it.

Again I say that The Kid's body lies undisturbed in the grave—and I speak of what I know.

ADDENDA.

The life of The Kid is ended, and my history thereof is finished. Perhaps, however, some of my readers will consent to follow me through three or four additional pages, which may be unnecessary and superfluous, but which I insert for my own personal gratification, and which I invite my friends to read.

During the time occupied in preparing the foregoing work for press, some circumstances have occurred, some newspaper articles have appeared, and many remarks have been passed, referring to the disposal of The Kid, his character, disposition, and history, and my contemplated publication of his life, which I have resolved to notice, against the advice of friends, who believe the proper and more dignified plan would be to ignore them altogether. But I have something to say, and propose to say it.

A San Francisco daily, in an article which I have never seen, but only comments thereon in other journals, among other strictures on my actions, questions my immunity from legal penalty for the slaying of The Kid. I did think I was fully advised in regard to this matter before I undertook the dangerous task of his re-arrest, as I contemplated the possible necessity of having to kill him. But I must acknowledge that I did not consult with the San Francisco editor, and can, at this late hour, only apologize, humbly, for the culpable omission. The law decided as to my amenability to its requirements—should the opinion of the scribbler be adverse, I can but abjectly crave his mercy.

I have been portrayed in print and in illustrations as shooting The Kid from behind a bed, from under a bed, and from other places of concealment. After mature deliberation I have resolved that honest confession will serve my purpose better than prevarication. Hear!

I was not behind the bed, because, in the first place, I could not get there. I'm not "as wide as a church door," but the bed was so close to the wall that a lath could scarce have been introduced between. I was not under the bed, and this fact will require a little more complicated explanation. I *could* have gotten under the bed; but, you see, I did not know The Kid was coming. He took me by surprise—gave me no chance on earth to hide myself. Had I but suspected his proximity, or that he would come upon me in that abrupt manner, I would have utilized any safe place of concealment which might have presented itself—under the bed, or under any article which I might have found under the bed, large enough to cover me.

Scared? Suppose a man of The Kid's noted gentle and amiable disposition and temper had warned you that when you two met you had better "come a shooting;" suppose he bounced in on you unexpectedly with a, revolver in his hand, whilst yours was in your scabbard. Scared? Wouldn't you have been scared? I didn't dare to answer his hail:—"*Quien es?*" as the first sound of my voice (which he knew perfectly well), would have been his signal to make a target of my physical personality, with his self-cocker, from which he was wont to pump a continuous stream of fire and lead, and in any direction, unerringly, which answered to his will. Scared, Cap? Well, I should say so. I started out on that expedition with the expectation of getting scared. I went out contemplating the probability of being shot at, and the possibility of being hurt, perhaps killed; but not if any precaution on my part would prevent such a catastrophe. The Kid got a very much better show than I had intended to give him.

Then, "the lucky shot," as they put it. It was not the shot, but the opportunity that was lucky, and everybody may rest assured I did not hesitate long to improve it. If there is any one simple enough to imagine that I did, or will *ever*, put my life squarely in the balance against that of The Kid, or any of his ilk, let him divest his mind of that absurd fallacy. It is said that Garrett did not give The Kid a fair show—did not fight him "on the square," etc. Whenever I take a contract to fight a man "on the square," as they put it (*par* parenthesis—I am not on the fight), that man must bear the reputation, before the world and in my estimation, of an honorable man and respectable citizen; or, at least, he must be my equal in social standing, and I claim the right to place my own estimate upon my own character, and my own evaluation upon my own life. If the public shall judge that these shall be measured by the same standard as those of outlaws and murderers, whose lives are forfeit to the law, I beg the privilege of appeal from its decision.

I had a hope—a very faint hope—of catching The Kid napping, as it were, so that I might disarm and capture him. Failing in that, my design was to try and get "the drop" on him, with the, almost, certainty, as I believed, that he would make good his threat to "die fighting with a revolver at each ear;" so with the drop, I would have been forced to kill him anyhow. I, at no time, contemplated taking any chances which I could avoid by caution or cunning. The only circumstances under which we could have met on equal terms, would have been accidental, and to which I would have been an unwilling party. Had we met unexpectedly, face to face, I have no idea that either one of us would have run away, and there is where the "square fight" would, doubtless, have come off. With one question I will dismiss the subject of taking unfair advantage, etc. What sort of "square fight," or "even show," would I have got, had one of The Kid's friends in Fort Sumner chanced to see me and informed him of my presence there and at Pete Maxwell's room on that fatal night?

A few words in regard to criticisms from two isolated rural journals published, I think, somewhere in the hilltops of the extreme northern counties of this Territory—at Guadalupitas, or Las Golondrinas, or La Cueva, or Vermejo. I have never seen a copy of either of them, and should have been ignorant of their existence had not a respectable newspaper copied their "puffs." These fellows objected to my writing and publishing a life of The Kid. Their expostulations come too late; it is written and I will quarrel before I abandon the design of publishing it.

One of these weekly emanations is called "The Optician," or some similar name, which would indicate that it is devoted to the interests of an industry which is, or should be, the exclusive prerogative of the disciples of Paul Pry. Perhaps it is a medical journal, edited by an M.D. who did not get the skull, nor the finger, nor any of the bones of The Kid's body, and is proportionately incensed thereat.

The other, judging from the two or three extracts I have seen from its columns, must, also, be a medical journal, published in the interests of an asylum for the imbeciles. I would advise the manager to exercise more vigilance in the absence of the editor and try to keep patients out of his chair. The unfortunate moonling who scribbled that "stickfull" which reflected upon me and my book, judging from his peculiar phraseology, must be a demented fishmonger.

You may spatter, you may soak him
With ink if you will,
But the scent of stale cat-fish
Will cling 'round him still.

Both of these delectable hermits charge me with intent to publish a life of The Kid, with the nefarious object of making money thereby. O! asinine propellers of Faber's No. 2; O! ludificatory lavishers of Arnold's night-tinted fluid; what the Hades else do you suppose my object could be? Their philosophy is that I must not attempt to make any more money out of the result of my "lucky shot," because, forsooth, "some men would have been satisfied," etc. Anybody, everybody else, authors who never were in New Mexico and never saw The Kid, can compile from newspaper rumors, as many lives of him as they please, make all the money out of their bogus, unreliable heroics that can be extorted from a gullible public, and these fellows will congratulate them; but my truthful history should be suppressed, because I got paid for ridding the country of a criminal. How do these impertinent intermeddlers know how much money I have made by this accident, or incident, or by whatever name they choose to designate it? How do they know how many thousands of dollars worth of stock and other property I have saved to those who "rewarded" me, by the achievement? Whose business is it if I choose to publish a hundred books, and make money out of them all, though I were as rich as the Harper Brothers? Wonder if either of these discontented fellows would have refused to publish my book on shares. Wonder what would have been the color of their notices, and when they would have "been satisfied." It's bile, Cully! nothing but bile. Take Indian Root Pills. And yet I thank you for your unsolicited, gratuitous notices, valueless as they are. They may help to sell a few copies of my work in your secluded locality. But, as I am no subject for charity (though your articles would seem to say so), send in reasonable bills and I will pay them. I know the difficulties under which projectors of newspapers in isolated regions labor, and would have sent you each a liberal advertisement without a hint, had I known of your existence.

It is amusing to notice how brave some of The Kid's "ancient enemies," and, even, some who professed to be his friends, have become since there is no danger of their courage being put to test by an interview with him. Some of them say that The Kid was a coward (which is a cowardly lie), and anybody, with any nerve, could have arrested him without trouble, thus obviating the necessity of killing him. One has seen him slapped in the face when he had a revolver in his hand, and he did not resent it. One has seen a Mexican, over on the Rio Grande, choke him against the wall, The Kid crying and begging with a cocked pistol in his hand. These blowers are unworthy of notice. Most of them were vagabonds who had "slopped" over from one faction to the other during the war, regulating their maneuvers according to the prospect of danger or safety, always keeping in view their chances to steal a sore-back pony or a speckled calf, and aspiring to the appellation of stock-owners. There is not one of these brave mouth-fighters that would have dared to give voice to such lying bravado whilst The Kid lived, though he were chained in a cell; not one of them that, were he on their track, would not have set the prairie on fire to get out of his reach, and, in their fright, extinguished it again as they ran, leaving a wet trail behind. These silly vaporings are but repeated illustrations of that old fable, "The Dead Lion and the Live Ass."

I will now take leave of all those of my readers who have not already taken "French leave" of me. Whatever may be the cause of the effect, Lincoln County now enjoys a season of peace and prosperity to which she has ever, heretofore, been a stranger. No Indians, no desperadoes, to scare our citizens from their labors, or disturb their slumbers. Stock wanders over the ranges in security, and vast fields of waving grain greet the eye, where, three years ago, not a stock of artificially-produced vegetation could be seen.

> "Where late was barrenness and waste,
> The perfumed blossom, bud and blade,
> Sweet, bashful pledges of approaching harvest,
> Giving cheerful promise to the hope of industry,"

Gladden the eye, stamp contentment on happy faces, and illustrate the pleasures of industry. The farmer to his plow, the stockman to his saddle, the merchant to his ledger, the blacksmith to his forge, the carpenter to his plane, the school-boy to his lass, and the shoemaker to his waxed-end, or *vice versa.*

The shoemaker to his | The schoolboy to his whackst
LAST END